341.23
JAC   Jacobs, William Jay

        Search for peace

SEARCH
for PEACE

SEARCH
for PEACE

The Story of the United Nations

WILLIAM JAY JACOBS

CHARLES SCRIBNER'S SONS • NEW YORK
Maxwell Macmillan Canada • Toronto
Maxwell Macmillan International
New York • Oxford • Singapore • Sydney

With deepest thanks for their help to the librarians of the Dag Hammarskjöld Library, United Nations Headquarters, New York.

Copyright © 1994 by William Jay Jacobs

Charles Scribner's Sons Books for Young Readers
Macmillan Publishing Company, 866 Third Avenue, New York, NY 10022

Maxwell Macmillan Canada, Inc.
1200 Eglinton Avenue East, Suite 200, Don Mills, Ontario M3C 3N1

Macmillan Publishing Company is part of
the Maxwell Communication Group of Companies.

First edition   10 9 8 7 6 5 4 3 2 1
Printed in the United States of America

Library of Congress Cataloging-in-Publication Data
Jacobs, William Jay.
Search for Peace : The story of the United Nations /
by William Jay Jacobs. — 1st ed.   p.   cm.
  Includes bibliographical references and index.
  ISBN 0-684-19652-2
1. United Nations—Juvenile literature.
2. Pacific settlement of international disputes—Juvenile literature.
   [1. United Nations.]   I. Title.
JX1977.Z8J28 1994   341.23—dc20   93-27149

SUMMARY: An overview of the United Nations: its formation, its successes and failures as international peacekeeper, the prospects for the future.

To the memory of
President Woodrow Wilson,
"Father of the Dream"...

They shall beat their swords into plowshares, and their spears into pruning-hooks: nation shall not lift up sword against nation, neither shall they learn war any more.

—ISAIAH 2.4
Engraved outside of United Nations Headquarters, New York

Contents

Foreword

On June 26, 1945, the Charter of the United Nations was signed. That charter declared a determination "to save succeeding generations from the scourge of war, which twice in our lifetime has brought untold sorrow to mankind. . . ."

The charter also reaffirmed the faith of member nations in "fundamental human rights" and in "the dignity and worth of the human person." Signing powers pledged "to practice tolerance and live together in peace with one another as good neighbors."

The United Nations, therefore, is an organization whose major purpose is to prevent nation-states from engaging in bloody conflict with one another. It is also pledged to protect individual human beings from mistreatment by governments.

For much of recorded history, the people of the world have lived under the rule of kings and queens or under governments made up of a small group of leaders holding great power.

Even today, thousands of years after such figures lived, we remember the names of powerful rulers in ancient Egypt—pharaohs like Ramses II and Amenhotep IV (Akhenaton), as well as such queens as Nefertiti and Hatshepsut. Yet at the bottom of

Sir A. Ramaswami Mudaliar, leader of the delegation from India, one of the fifty nations represented at the San Francisco Conference in 1945, signs the Charter of the United Nations on behalf of his country. *United Nations Photo.*

the Egyptian pyramid of social classes, holding almost no power, were the great majority of the people—the peasant farmers and slaves who were forced to do the society's hard work while being given barely enough food, clothing, and shelter to survive.

We also know of the Roman emperor, Caesar Augustus, who brought peace and order to his great empire, which stretched from the Atlantic Ocean to the Euphrates River and from Scotland to the Black Sea. But in Rome, too, men eventually came into authority who did not bring their people goodness or happiness. Instead they brought selfishness and war. They brought confusion, a continuing struggle for influence, and a craving for glory. To display their own importance they spent the public's money wildly, stupidly.

During the early 1700s in France, King Louis XIV held total command. Once, when asked to speak about the government of the French nation, he replied firmly, *"L'état c'est moi"*: "I am the state [government]." The reign of Louis XIV is often cited as an example of how much a truly strong ruler can accomplish in one lifetime. Yet Louis also brought with his time as king a series of wars, of persecution, and of poverty for much of the population. Thus, when he died, the people of France openly celebrated.

In the twentieth century, our own century, we have seen some of the mightiest governments in all of human history. Often they have been led by ruthless dictators—men who held the power of life and death over citizens in their countries, very much as the pharaohs once did in ancient Egypt.

In Russia, for example, Vladimir Ilyich Lenin, Leon Trotsky, and Joseph Stalin seized power from a line of rulers known as czars. The new Russian leaders claimed to "serve the people." They promised to make a better life for even the very poor by dividing up the nation's wealth. But their experiment failed. The economy did not work. Meanwhile, Joseph Stalin had millions of people killed to assure himself total control. He seized the territories of neighboring countries and led the way for Soviet influence in such distant lands as Vietnam and even Cuba—near the coast of the Soviet's greatest foe, the United States of America.

During the 1930s Adolf Hitler seized power in Germany. One of the cruelest men who ever lived, he set up special camps for the sole purpose of killing enemies or those he considered

racially inferior—Jews, Gypsies, socialists—anybody who did not
like him or who might put limits on his ambition for complete
control over the people of Europe. The combined might of all the
armies of the free world was finally required to defeat him.

Clearly, there are people who choose to follow such leaders
out of fear for their own safety. In the days of the cave dwellers,
there was the danger of being clubbed to death or of being
dragged away by the hair as a captive to somebody's cave.
Without a strong government there is uncertainty, confusion.
There can be what the political thinker Thomas Hobbes once
called "a state of nature" or "a war of all against all."

Strong leaders, including the brutal dictators of modern
times, know that by using an army and a police force they can
create a sense of order, of safety, in the minds of those they rule.
Such rulers can make people feel part of something bigger than
themselves—a state that will live on after they themselves have
died. They can unite with their friends and neighbors against
people who are different from them in race, or religion, or ap-
pearance. They can raise their arms together in a shared salute,
such as "*Heil* Hitler!" Their lives, therefore, can have a sense of
meaning, purpose, direction.

The result, especially in the twentieth century, has been almost constant bloody warfare—race against race, religion against
religion, nation against nation. Hindus and Muslims kill each
other in India. Serbs, Croats, and Bosnians kill one another in
what, a short time ago, was Yugoslavia. Communists kill non-
Communists in Cambodia.

Must it always be so? Must children in coming centuries be
doomed to lives of suffering and pain, taking up arms against
their neighbors?

Or is there another way to live? Can we learn to come together on this planet: to respect one another's differences, to grow from one another's knowledge? Can we, at last, truly become a world community sharing the experience of "life, liberty, and the pursuit of happiness"?

The answers to those questions still are uncertain. But they are central to our own lives and to the lives of our children and grandchildren and beyond. They are central to human existence.

And that is what this book is all about—and what the United Nations is all about. Few topics are of such absolute, such monumental importance.

Flags of some of the member nations fly outside the United Nations building in New York. *United Nations Photo 57106.*

1

Centuries of Conflict and the Dream of the League of Nations

The dream of a world united against the awful wastes of war is . . . deeply imbedded in the hearts of men everywhere.

—*WOODROW WILSON*

War.

War has been central to the story of the human race on this planet. Some of the oldest records of humanity are filled with accounts of battles and of killing. The people of the ancient Middle East, including the advanced, sophisticated Egyptians, fought many wars. So did the inhabitants of the cities of classical Greece, such as Athens and Sparta.

Alexander the Great became known as "great" because of his spectacular military victories.

Rome, first in the days of the Republic and then in the centuries of the Empire, achieved power through the use of force.

The story of the Middle Ages is familiar to us primarily through suits of armor, swords, and the great castles and military fortresses that still survive today. Medieval tales that we read in books tell of gallant knights—warriors who risked their lives in quest of victory in combat.

The Renaissance, it is true, survives for us in extraordinary works of art. Yet we know it, too, because of the cruelty and bloodshed described in such works as the autobiography of Benvenuto Cellini. Similarly, we glorify the remarkable art of Leonardo da Vinci. But history also remembers him as the ingenious inventor of weapons whose principles are still copied in the twentieth century. Finally, Renaissance literature lives on in such works as Niccolò Machiavelli's *The Prince*—a book of advice dedicated to helping rulers stay in power through the use of force and fear.

The Renaissance gave way to the modern world and to the rise of larger nation-states. Such modern nations came into being primarily because of their greater economic power and their capacity to compete for survival in time of war.

From the sixteenth through the twentieth centuries such nations as France, England, Russia, Japan, Germany, and the United States engaged in greater and greater struggles. In World War II, the total casualties numbered more than fifty-five million people killed and wounded, millions of those in horrible concentration camps.

Such numbers could actually appear small compared to what might happen next if nuclear devices are ever used again, such as the atomic bombs dropped by the United States on Hiroshima and Nagasaki, Japan, in August 1945. Since that time, incredibly sophisticated weapons have been developed by world powers— tools of death capable of destroying much, if not all, of human civilization.

Throughout history there have been valiant attempts to put an end to war—to assure lasting peace. Many of those efforts have

Two brothers who survived the Nagasaki bomb. *United Nations Photo 149450 / Yosuke Yamahata.*

been based on religion. Some six centuries before the birth of Jesus, the followers of Gautama Buddha dedicated themselves to the elimination of acts of violence by human beings against one another. So, too, did the monarch of India, Asoka, as well as the Essenes of ancient Palestine. But those experiments produced little success of a lasting kind.

It was Jesus of Nazareth who urged his followers to "turn the other cheek" after experiencing violence against their bodies. Later, however, some of the most prominent Christian leaders, such as St. Augustine and St. Thomas Aquinas, argued that war itself is sometimes necessary to bring about the triumph of the Christian religion and to achieve a lasting peace.

Such a view is still commonly held today in Christian countries that arm local police forces with deadly weapons in order to assure the triumph of "law and order."

Particularly in the last six centuries there have been important nonreligious, attempts to assure a lasting peace among the world's people. Great writers such as the poet Dante described the need for a world government. So, too, did insightful political figures and commentators including William Penn, Jean-Jacques Rousseau, and Immanuel Kant.

The brilliant French monarch Henry IV managed not only to triumph and to unite all of France in the early 1600s, but to suggest a plan known to history as the Grand Design. In proposing a form of government that would assure lasting peace for a united world, it was an idea far ahead of its time. The world was not yet ready for so bold a scheme.

With the defeat of Napoléon Bonaparte and the calling of the Congress of Vienna in 1815, there began a century of relative peace and order in the world. Yet even that period was interrupted by European revolutionary struggles in 1830 and 1848, the Crimean War (dealt with at the Congress of Paris in 1856), and later conflicts relating to the unification of Italy and Germany.

Still, the Hague Conferences of 1899 and 1907 showed that even major disputes between nations could sometimes be settled peacefully.

On June 28, 1914, Archduke Francis Ferdinand of Austria was assassinated in Sarajevo by Serbian nationalists. Within a month, the system of alliances then in effect came into play and World War I began. Despite all the political institutions in operation since the defeat of Napoléon a century earlier, no single organization proved strong enough to prevent the outbreak of the terrible conflict.

As the war finally neared its conclusion, President Woodrow Wilson of the United States began to work for the creation of a world organization that could help to prevent future conflicts. In June 1919 the Treaty of Versailles finally ended World War I.

One provision of that treaty called for the creation of the League of Nations, an organization whose major purpose was to prevent the outbreak of similar conflicts in the future. The League was intended to help nations work together for world peace and security.

President Wilson looked forward to "such a concert of free peoples as shall bring peace and safety to all nations."

To achieve its goals, the League created four major divisions for its operation: the General Assembly, the Council, the Secretariat, and the Permanent Court of International Justice.

The General Assembly included all members of the organi-

An oil painting by British artist George Sheridan Knowles portrays President Woodrow Wilson reading his opening address to the Peace Conference in Paris, January 18, 1919. *The Art Museum, Princeton University. Gift of Charles K. Lock. Photograph by Taylor & Dull, Inc.*

zation, each of them represented equally. The Council was to include the five victorious "great powers"—the United States, Great Britain, France, Italy, and Japan, with other nations to be elected for temporary service.

The Secretariat, headed by a secretary-general, was to carry out the administrative duties of the League. And the court was to handle various kinds of disputes among nations that during the previous century had been dealt with by a wide variety of world bodies.

In order to achieve victory in the terrible conflict, nations had been brought together in a successful alliance. But in the peacetime world that followed, serious problems arose almost from the very beginning. The United States Congress, for example, refused to permit President Wilson's own country to join the League.

Meanwhile, the Russian Revolution, led by Vladimir Ilyich Lenin, brought Communists to power in that country and, until 1934, caused the League to close its doors to their newly formed Union of Soviet Socialist Republics. Germany, defeated in World War I, was not admitted to membership in the world body until 1926.

What were the goals of League of Nations members? By and large, the triumphant Allied nations of Europe were determined to make the most of their victory—one expensive both in money and in blood. To them, it seemed an opportunity to shape the future, to determine what would happen in world affairs.

Woodrow Wilson had an altogether different dream. Like most of the common people of Western Europe and of the United States, he hoped to end the continuing conflicts among nations—to establish a lasting peace on the planet. So idealistic a goal was based on a democratic view of people and their governments.

According to Wilson, nations must be servants of the world's people, not their masters. They must practice "open diplomacy" instead of making secret deals behind closed doors. And they must be highly moral in dealing with issues that could lead to war.

Further, Wilson believed that if "outlaws" arose, the League and its members should be sufficiently powerful and united to deal with such criminals. Yet, since he assumed that most people are essentially good—not evil—he believed that most problems could be solved through discussion rather than through warfare.

The League, then, would be a rather remarkable kind of civilized "club," where nations could face issues rationally and responsibly, settling them without war.

As did Woodrow Wilson, most of the founders of the League recognized that "accidents" sometimes happened and, in the past, wars had broken out. But never before had there been an organization such as the League of Nations. With that new body, they believed, it would be possible to deal with future conflicts between national alliances. Warfare would no longer be necessary.

Nations would still exist as nations, said the founders of the League. But wars would never again take place while the rest of humanity simply looked the other way, uncaring and unfeeling. Warfare anywhere would be a matter of worldwide concern.

History, unfortunately, failed to follow the vision of the League's founders.

The United States never joined the world body.

When, in 1933, Japan was condemned for seizing Manchuria and attacking China, the Japanese resigned their membership.

Germany, under the ruthless dictatorship of Adolf Hitler, also withdrew in 1933, only seven years after being admitted to the organization.

So, too, did Italy, in 1937, after the League condemned Benito Mussolini's seizure of Ethiopia.

Finally, when the Soviet Union, led by Joseph Stalin, attacked Finland in 1939, the League of Nations formally expelled the Soviet state.

When Hitler's Nazi troops invaded Poland in September 1939, World War II began.

The League had failed in its primary mission—keeping the world at peace.

Still, in the two decades since its birth, the organization had done important things. The Permanent Court of International Justice, located in The Hague, Netherlands, settled several important cases brought to it by member nations. Meanwhile, Sir Eric Drummond of England, serving from 1920 to 1933 as the League's first secretary-general, demonstrated that a well-organized team of international specialists could make a significant difference in world affairs. Membership in the world body finally reached a peak of fifty-eight nations.

The principal problem, however, was that France and Great Britain, the League's two major powers, proved too badly hurt by the Great Depression of the 1930s—and too weak in their elected leadership—to stand up against the aggression of Germany, Italy, Japan, and the Soviet Union.

While the League's Council and General Assembly sometimes were able to address disputes between weaker nations, such as Sweden and Finland, or Greece and Bulgaria, they were unable to stop the aggressive moves of the dictators—Hitler, Mussolini, Tojo, and Stalin—men who had little respect for the strength of the League of Nations.

And so, World War II came to be.

2

World War II and the Formation of the United Nations

We appeal as human beings to human beings:
Remember your humanity and forget the rest.

—*ALBERT EINSTEIN*

When the League of Nations was first created, President Woodrow Wilson declared, "A living thing is born." But the United States never joined the League. And it may well be that World War II occurred because dictators, like Adolf Hitler, came to believe they had nothing to fear from the world's weak, disorganized democracies.

Thus, speaking after the United States finally entered the Second World War, Cordell Hull, secretary of state under President Franklin Delano Roosevelt, blamed his own nation for not previously taking part in the enforcement of world peace.

America was at war against Germany, Italy, and Japan, said Hull, "because we ignored the simple but fundamental truth that the price of peace . . . is the acceptance of international responsibilities."

In the future, he declared, a new international organization would have to use armed force when necessary for the "regulation of armaments [and] . . . settlement of disputes between nations." America therefore must "throw [its] moral and international influence in the direction of creating a stable and enduring order under law."

Clearly, as many had come to believe, some kind of world organization was necessary.

In August 1941 President Roosevelt met on shipboard off the coast of Newfoundland with Prime Minister Winston Churchill of Great Britain. The two leaders produced an important historical document: the Atlantic Charter.

Among its critical points were promises that, following an Allied victory, the world's nations would work together for peace, that people everywhere would have an opportunity for jobs and for economic security after retirement, and that a new system should be created to assure world order.

To make certain that Congress would not once again reject membership for the United States in an organization dedicated to world peace, President Roosevelt took action. He worked closely with prominent Republican party figures such as Senator Arthur Vandenberg, along with Democrats, including Senator J. William Fulbright.

Before long, Congress adopted by an overwhelming vote a resolution calling for the participation of the United States in "the creation of . . . international machinery, with powers adequate to establish and to maintain a joint and lasting peace among nations of the world."

Soon afterward, Wendell L. Willkie, Roosevelt's Republican opponent in the presidential election of 1940, wrote a deeply moving book entitled *One World* in support of such international cooperation.

In October 1943, the foreign ministers of Great Britain, the Soviet Union, China, and the United States met in Moscow. They signed what is known to history as the Declaration of Moscow, urging the creation of a new international organization dedicated to preserving world peace, based on "the equality of all peace-loving states."

Then, in late November and early December 1943, President Roosevelt and Prime Minister Churchill met with Marshal Joseph Stalin in Tehran, Iran.

On their way to the Tehran Conference, Roosevelt and Churchill had met with the Chinese leader, Chiang Kai-shek. The three agreed that all of the lands conquered by Japan would be taken away from that aggressor and that Korea, then under Japanese control, would be made a free and independent nation.

The most important result of the Tehran Conference was an agreement that, following victory, a "United Nations" organization would "make a peace which will command the goodwill of the overwhelming masses of the people of the world and banish the scourge and terror of war. . . ."

As President Roosevelt later said in a radio broadcast to the American people following his return from Tehran, "As long as the four nations [the U.S., Great Britain, the Soviet Union, and China] stick together in determination to keep peace, there will be no possibility of an aggressor nation raising another war."

In planning for the creation of the United Nations organization, the most important sessions took place from late August to early October 1944 at Dumbarton Oaks, a stately mansion near Washington, D.C.

Serious, sometimes even angry, debates erupted at the Dumbarton Oaks Conference among delegates of the same four great powers attending the sessions there.

On one stormy issue in particular, no agreement could be reached among the participants. The Soviet Union demanded for all four major powers (later five with the addition of France) the right to veto (reject) any decision on peacekeeping actions taken by the United Nations Security Council. That crucial group was permanently to include the major powers and a rotating group of six (now ten) smaller nations.

The Soviets also demanded separate voting membership for all sixteen republics of the Union of Soviet Socialist Republics in the General Assembly of the United Nations, where all member nations of the organization were included. In response to that demand, President Roosevelt jokingly proposed that each of the then forty-eight states of the United States should also have a separate vote.

Despite those unresolved matters, the Dumbarton Oaks Conference did agree on some basic features of the new international organization, the United Nations. Most important, it was decided that, in addition to the Security Council and General Assembly, other basic organs of the U.N. would include an international court of justice, an economic and social council, and a secretariat, headed by a secretary-general. (All are administrative units discussed in chapter 3 of this book.)

The serious issues left unsettled at Dumbarton Oaks were discussed again by Roosevelt, Churchill, and Stalin in February 1945 at Yalta, a resort area in the Crimea, formerly popular with wealthy Russian aristocrats.

At Yalta it was decided that, as the Soviets had demanded, each of the five permanent members of the Security Council—the United States, the USSR, Great Britain, China, and France— would be given the right to veto matters brought before the Security Council. As a compromise, it was also decided that two large republics of the Soviet Union, the Ukraine and Byelorussia, would be granted full membership status in the United Nations— not all sixteen republics as the Soviets had originally proposed.

With those compromises, the major task that lay ahead for the member states was to prepare a charter—a constitution—for their new organization. That task was to be addressed at a meeting scheduled for April 25, 1945, in San Francisco.

On April 12, however, the president of the United States, Franklin Delano Roosevelt, died. Scarcely an hour after being sworn in as his successor, Harry S. Truman announced that the conference would proceed as scheduled. It was Truman himself who had the honor of calling the opening session to order.

By the time of the San Francisco conference, few issues remained to be resolved. Many critical matters had already been given voice in the Atlantic Charter, the Tehran Declaration, the Dumbarton Oaks meeting, and the Yalta Declaration. Still, it required two months of discussion to draft the Charter of the United Nations—in sharp contrast to the thirty hours needed to prepare the Covenant of the League of Nations.

On June 25, 1945, the delegates of fifty nations signed the newly written charter. On October 24 the document formally went into effect.

The United Nations, an organization dedicated to preserving peace on earth, had become a reality.

Even now, half a century after the United Nations was created in San Francisco, it probably is too early to know what kind of organization it will eventually become. Yet we can clearly see why some things happened as they did in 1945.

Not long after World War II began, Secretary of State Cordell Hull of the United States had begun planning with British officials for a stronger form of international organization to replace the League of Nations. As the war progressed, a variety of agencies were organized to deal with potential problems. Among them were the United Nations Relief and Rehabilitation Administration (UNRRA), the Food and Agriculture Organization (FAO), and the International Monetary Fund (IMF).

Other United Nations bodies were built directly on League of Nations institutions. The Permanent Court of International Justice, for example, descended directly from the League's World Court. In that sense, the United Nations often put into practice ideas and policies that could be traced back in history an entire century or more.

Also like the League, the United Nations owed much to an American president, in this case Franklin Delano Roosevelt. Roosevelt's worldwide popularity made a contribution similar to Woodrow Wilson's idealism in the founding of the earlier body. The U.N. Charter reflects the commitment of both American leaders to such causes as human rights.

Still, those who organized the United Nations were careful to portray it to the world as a *new* organization, not just an extension or a copy of the League of Nations. In its location (New York City) and in its original personnel, there was a conscious effort to demonstrate that the United Nations would mark a fresh start in working toward world peace.

The first delegation from the United States was also very much concerned with some of the broader tasks to be performed by the United Nations. As in the case of UNESCO (the United Nations Educational, Scientific, and Cultural Organization), it

Prime Minister Clement Attlee of Great Britain addresses the first session of the United Nations General Assembly at Central Hall in London, January 10, 1946. *United Nations Photo 24507 / Marcel Bolomey.*

was hoped that dealing boldly with such matters—social, humanitarian, and cultural—would make the United Nations significant to *all* of humanity, not just to leaders concerned with politics and the military.

At the same time, however, the Charter of the United Nations made it clear that the organization was not originally intended to be a world government. It was to be based on the *cooperation* of its members, not their transformation into a superstate or "world order."

Even those delegates who believed in world government understood that by trying to go too far, too fast, they might cause people in some nations to turn against the idea of the United Nations itself. The great powers also understood that they could not create an organization so powerful that it would dominate all the lesser nations of the world.

The founders of the United Nations knew, too, that international situations change. The alliance that had defeated the Axis powers (Germany, Italy, and Japan) might not survive. Indeed, with the growing certainty of an Allied victory over Germany, it had become increasingly clear that the Soviet Union had ambitions of its own. Thus the United States was at first concerned that providing the five major nations in the Security Council—including the USSR—with individual veto power might make the United Nations practically useless in times of real crisis.

Since the United Nations was formed, the defeated powers of Germany and Japan have once again become rich and powerful, while the Soviet Union has been dismembered into separate national parts, its various republics functioning with considerable independence from Mother Russia.

A final comparison with the League of Nations: While the Charter of the United Nations in many ways is similar to the Covenant of the League of Nations, it also is quite different. Most importantly, the United Nations provides far more specialized agencies, whose task is to deal with the political, economic, and social factors that give rise to war.

Examples of such agencies are: the World Health Organization (WHO); the International Monetary Fund (IMF); the Food and Agriculture Organization (FAO); the International Labor Organization (ILO); and the United Nations Educational, Scientific, and Cultural Organization (UNESCO). In addition, the U.N. General Assembly's Economic and Social Council includes such groups as the United Nations International Children's Emergency Fund (UNICEF).

Even during periods of bitter conflict between the "Communist world" and the "free world," the U.N. agencies were committed to activities intended to remove the *causes* of war.

In the beginning, and for many years after the United Nations was founded, it probably was impossible to address with strength some of the basic problems of life on planet Earth: the organization of a standing army to deal with crises between nations or within a single nation, arms control and disarmament, and specific methods for protecting human rights. At the San Francisco Conference in 1945 and for almost four decades afterward, international rivalries prevented the United Nations from developing mechanisms to face such issues.

It was too soon.

Yet what was done in the beginning, so many years ago, may well prove to be of enormous significance from the perspective of history. On one level, it may simply mean that nation-states will be better able to deal with international problems.

But beyond that, it perhaps may mean that some kind of world government eventually may emerge. And if such an international structure really does develop, the result could well be, as predicted in the Bible, that "nation shall not lift up sword against nation, neither shall they learn war any more."

3

How the United Nations Is Structured

> If we do not want to die together in war, we must learn to live together in peace.
>
> —*Harry S. Truman*

There is little doubt about the objectives of the United Nations. The organization is ultimately intended to eliminate the continuing horror of international conflict—war. It is committed to the rule of law and justice, as well as to social progress and human rights.

To achieve those crucial objectives, the United Nations is organized into six principal organs: the General Assembly, the Security Council, the Economic and Social Council, the Trusteeship Council, the International Court of Justice, and the Secretariat.

In addition, there are some twenty smaller specialized agencies, many of them working closely with one or more of the major bodies. Others deal with very specific tasks, such as the World Health Organization (WHO), the International Monetary Fund (IMF), and the Food and Agriculture Organization (FAO).

Not all of the six major U.N. organs are equal in their power. Both the Economic and Social Council and the Trusteeship Council, for example, report to the General Assembly, which gives them direction. The Secretariat and its leader, the U.N. secretary-general, also report to the General Assembly. But the Secretariat has certain specialized powers of crucial importance that are independent of the General Assembly.

Because of the complexity of the United Nations, it is useful to examine its various component parts individually to gain a clearer overview of what they do.

The General Assembly

In many ways the General Assembly is the central unit of the United Nations. Each member nation of the world body is represented in it with one vote. Any issue that concerns the U.N. can be debated in the General Assembly—even questions of peace and war. Because it is so all-inclusive in its membership, the General Assembly can be seen as the "world parliament" or the "town meeting of the world."

Powers of the General Assembly

Under the United Nations Charter, the powers of the General Assembly are:

• To discuss any matter, regardless of how large or small, relating to international security (except those being debated at the same time by the Security Council) and to make recommendations on those issues.

• To consider questions concerning armament and disarmament among nations of the world.

• To consider matters relating to any of the other organs of the United Nations.

• To choose the ten nonpermanent members of the Security Council, as well as the members of the Economic and Social Council. The General Assembly also selects those members of the Trusteeship Council who are elected. Along with the Security Council, it chooses the judges of the International Court of Justice. It is the assembly, too, on the recommendation of the Security Council, that chooses the U.N. secretary-general.

• To receive reports from all of the other U.N. organs, including the Security Council.

• To coordinate the work of the various U.N. agencies on such matters as international law and human rights. The General Assembly makes certain that efforts in the economic, social, cultural, educational, and health fields are shared between groups such as the Economic and Social Council and the United Nations Children's Fund.

• To develop a budget for the United Nations and decide how much money each member nation will contribute to the organization.

Finally, since November 1950, the General Assembly has had the power to act independently when the Security Council, faced with military aggression somewhere in the world, does not have the approval of all five permanent members of the council.

That so-called uniting-for-peace power first came about when the Soviet Union did not approve of U.N. aid for South Korea, which had been invaded by Soviet-supported North Korea. uniting-for-peace power was used again during the Suez crisis of 1956 and the conflict in the Congo in 1960.

Sessions of the General Assembly

The General Assembly meets formally every year from late in September until mid-December. But it may also meet in special sessions within twenty-four hours after the request of nine members of the Security Council, or by a majority vote of the assembly's member nations.

Operations of the General Assembly

At the beginning of each formal session, the assembly elects its own president, along with twenty-one vice-presidents and the chairpersons of its seven main committees (including committees on such matters as disarmament; decolonization; social, humanitarian, and cultural matters; as well as legal and financial issues).

It is those committees that carry on the work of the General Assembly during the approximately nine months of the year when the assembly is not in session. Work also has been conducted by committees set up to deal with specific problems, such as exploration of outer space or apartheid (national laws in South Africa intended to keep people separated by race). Sometimes, too, there are international conferences organized by the assembly on matters raised by the secretary-general and his or her staff.

Taken together, the tremendous amount of work engaged in by organs of the General Assembly have a common goal: to achieve world peace and improved personal conditions for the earth's people.

It is true that the assembly's debates sometimes appear to be long, self-serving arguments on the part of individual member nations. But what ultimately is at stake is the achievement of goals at the very heart of the reason for forming a United Nations organization in the first place.

The Security Council

The Security Council is the organ of the United Nations given primary responsibility for maintaining world peace. The council now has fifteen members: five permanent members—the United States, Russia, Great Britain, France, and China—and ten nations elected by the General Assembly for terms of two years.

Powers of the Security Council

Among the powers of the Security Council provided in the United Nations Charter are:

• To investigate any international dispute that might lead to war and then to recommend ways to settle that dispute.
• To prevent or put an end to aggression by calling on members to take economic action against offending nations.
• To take actual military action against aggressor nations.
• To be certain that the responsibilities of the United Nations in trusteeship countries are actually carried out.
• To nominate candidates for secretary-general, as well as to share responsibility with the General Assembly for choosing the judges of the International Court of Justice.

Representatives of the Security Council's member nations must be present at U.N. headquarters in New York at all times. When a problem arises, the council will usually try to settle it peacefully. But then, if negotiation fails, the council is entitled to send peacekeeping forces to help bring about new negotiations or to separate the warring parties.

There may also be economic sanctions, such as blocking trade with a nation. If all else fails, the Security Council may use

The Security Council votes in November 1990 to use "all necessary means" to compel Iraq to withdraw from Kuwait. *United Nations Photo 177113 / Milton Grant.*

actual military force, as in the case of Cambodia and other countries in the early 1990s.

For more than four decades, bitter competition took place between the Soviet Union, China, and their Communist-bloc allies against the United States and other nations of the "free world." During those years the actions of the Security Council were often blocked by the threat of vetoes by the five permanent members of the council—all of whom actually used their power of the veto at various times.

Since the waning of conflict in the Cold War, however, the

potential power of the Security Council to act decisively in international crises has grown considerably. During the Persian Gulf War of 1991, for example, the United States and Russia worked together with other powerful nations to help bring a rapid and decisive end to the conflict.

Clearly then, in times of international crisis it is the Security Council that must carry the greatest responsibility for action if the United Nations truly is to succeed in achieving peace.

The decisions of that council, even today, are dominated by the world's most powerful nations.

The Economic and Social Council

The Economic and Social Council of the United Nations (ECOSOC) is concerned with crucial matters relating to the causes of war and productive ways to assure lasting peace. Originally, ECOSOC had eighteen members, but as the United Nations grew, ECOSOC also grew, so that it now includes representatives of fifty-four nations.

Each year the General Assembly elects eighteen members to serve for a three-year term, with reelection possible at the end of three years. As a matter of practice, all five permanent members of the Security Council serve on a continuing basis.

The major work of the Economic and Social Council is to report on economic, social, cultural, educational, and health-related matters. It is also concerned with such problems as human rights, narcotics dealing, and the treatment of women around the world.

ECOSOC works closely with several so-called specialized agencies, related to the United Nations by standing agreement, although they have their own managers and their own budgets. Those groups include, for example:

The International Labor Organization (ILO)
The Food and Agriculture Organization of the United Nations (FAO)
The United Nations Educational, Scientific, and Cultural Organization (UNESCO)
The World Health Organization (WHO)
The International Monetary Fund (IMF).

In addition, more than six hundred specialized nongovernmental organizations consult with ECOSOC. They may attend meetings of the council and submit advisory papers to it. Those groups are entitled to consult with the U.N. Secretariat on matters of shared concern.

The Economic and Social Council receives little of the publicity enjoyed by United Nations military forces sent into battle against aggressors. Still, ECOSOC bodies play a critical role in striking out against the underlying causes of war. In the future that role may become even more important.

The Trusteeship Council

During the years when the League of Nations was alive, the world included many territories under the so-called protection of colonial powers. Even when the United Nations was formed, there still were eleven so-called Trust Territories, supervised by seven U.N. member nations and containing approximately twenty million people.

Today, only one small part of those eleven territories is still under the supervision of a U.N. member. The others, most of them in Africa, are all either independent nations or have joined with neighboring countries.

The last remaining Trust Territory is Belau, once part of the Trust Territory of the Pacific Islands, supervised by the United States. That territory, known as Micronesia, formerly included more than 2,100 islands clustered into three groups: the Marianas, the Carolines, and the Marshalls—altogether some 133,000 people.

In December 1990 the Security Council declared that the trusteeship of those islands had fully achieved its purposes and no longer was necessary. Only tiny Belau is still classified as a "strategic area," administered by the United States.

Among the other Trust Territories, British Togoland, for example, joined with the neighboring Gold Coast to form the independent nation of Ghana, now a regular member of the United Nations. The former French colonies of Togo and the French Cameroons also became independent.

Meanwhile, the British Cameroons later split apart: the Northern Cameroons voting to join with Nigeria, the Southern Cameroons deciding to join with the former French Cameroons to form a nation known today as Cameroon.

Perhaps the most tragic fate among former colonies is that of the nation of Somalia, organized from the former Italian and British territories of Somaliland. In 1992 Somalia became the setting for United Nations intervention, spearheaded by troops from the United States, when tribal fighting among clans became so vicious that virtually all order in the nation broke down, giving way to bloody warfare.

Clearly, however, the old era of colonialism has ended—the

time when League of Nations and U.N. mechanisms were needed to care for former colonies. No matter how weak they may be, such territories now are free and independent national units in today's world.

With the work of the Trusteeship Council largely completed, some have suggested that it focus primarily on the burning issue of the self-determination of people—the movement toward democracy in nations that once were colonies. Others have suggested that in coming years the Trusteeship Council should specialize in problems of the environment.

What is certain is that the issue of "trust territories," a major problem at the beginning of the twentieth century, has now largely disappeared.

International Court of Justice

The International Court of Justice actually is a continuation of the Permanent Court of International Justice, an organ of the old League of Nations.

Located in The Hague, Netherlands, it is made up of fifteen judges, each of them from a different country. Judges are chosen jointly by the General Assembly and by the Security Council. Once elected, the judges are to serve for nine years and may be reelected. Usually the court has included one judge from each of the five great powers.

No nation is forced to submit a case to the court, but the Security Council can recommend to nations in conflict that a legal problem be decided by it. Both the Security Council and the General Assembly may ask the court for advisory opinions on legal matters.

In making its decisions the International Court of Justice does not apply the standards of justice used by any one particular country or group of countries. Instead, its judgments are based on international custom and "the general principles of law recognized by civilized nations."

As of now, fewer than half the members of the United Nations have ever agreed to submit cases for the court to decide. When the United States and Israel brought cases concerning planes shot down by former Soviet-bloc countries—including the Soviet Union, Hungary, and Bulgaria—those nations refused to accept the right of the court to judge.

In some recent years the court has had only one or two cases brought before it and, even then, nations occasionally have refused to accept the body's decision.

So far the most important contributions of the International Court of Justice have been in advisory opinions given to specialized agencies of the United Nations on certain complex legal matters.

It has been suggested that if governments continue to ignore the court as a means for settling their disputes, it should be disbanded. Yet, given the strong legal history of nations such as Great Britain and the United States, it seems unlikely that the United Nations could ever build a stable, peaceful arena of world politics without a more certain, dependable, predictable legal system—one that actually works and is *used*.

The Secretariat

If the Secretariat were just an administrative unit serving the United Nations, it would not be appropriate to discuss it in a

chapter on how the world body is organized. In practice, however, it is far more important. The Secretariat and its chief offi-
cer, the secretary-general, go well beyond just preparing for
meetings, distributing papers, hiring staff, and operating the
U.N. library.

True, the secretary-general has considerable administrative
responsibility. He heads an international staff of more than
twenty-five thousand workers from over 150 countries. He is in
charge of daily activities at U.N. headquarters in New York and
in offices around the globe. His employees are charged with the
tasks of translating documents, preparing U.N. publications, and
operating information centers—matters relating to administrative
detail.

But the secretary-general and his staff also have much
broader responsibilities. They prepare studies on crucial economic and social trends and problems. They investigate matters
relating to disarmament, military weapons development, and
human rights. Finally, they are charged with crucial diplomatic
and political tasks, including the administration—and sometimes
the launching—of armed peacekeeping operations against aggressors.

Some holders of the position of secretary-general have been
exceptionally strong in their handling of peacekeeping. One of
them, Dag Hammarskjöld, so angered Soviet premier Nikita
Khrushchev that the Soviet leader proposed a total restructuring
of the secretary-generalship. It should immediately become, said
Khrushchev, a "troika" (a carriage drawn by three horses)—three
leaders, representing the Communist world, the Western world,
and neutral states.

The Khrushchev suggestion gained almost no support in the
United Nations outside his own bloc of nations. What he clearly

Trygve Lie of Norway (1945–1952). *United Nations Photo 1416.*

Dag Hammarskjöld of Sweden (1953–1961). *United Nations Photo / ES.*

U Thant of Burma (1961–1971). *United Nations Photo 92603 / Y. Nagata.*

Kurt Waldheim of Austria (1972–1981). *United Nations Photo / D. Burnett.*

Javier Pérez de Cuéllar of Peru (1982–1991). *United Nations Photo 159681 / J. Isaac.*

Boutros Boutros-Ghali of Egypt (1992—). *United Nations Photo 178980 / M. Grant.*

had hoped to do was eliminate the possible growth of leadership strength for any official in the world organization.

Since the founding of the United Nations in 1945, six men have held the position of secretary-general. Trygve Lie of Norway served from the organization's founding until 1952. His successor, Dag Hammarskjöld of Sweden, held office from 1953 until his death in a plane crash in 1961 while on a U.N. mission in Africa.

U Thant of Burma then served until 1971. He, in turn, was followed by Kurt Waldheim of Austria, who occupied the position from 1972 through 1981. Javier Pérez de Cuéllar of Peru served from 1982 until 1991, when Boutros Boutros-Ghali of Egypt became the organization's secretary-general.

Because of the fading of Cold War tension between Communist countries and the West, it is the last of these leaders, Boutros Boutros-Ghali, who may well have the greatest opportunity to achieve objectives that cut across the narrow goals of individual nations and blocs of nations. He may be able to take important steps toward a more truly united world.

A Note on the Budget of the United Nations

Every two years the U.N. secretary-general submits a budget to the General Assembly. Those budget figures are then reviewed by a committee of specialists before being voted on by the assembly.

The United Nations budget for 1992–1993 amounted to $1,940,000,000, which meant expenditures of $2,389,000,000 minus income estimates of $449,000,000.

Funds came largely from contributions by member states on a scale based on ability to pay. According to current practice, no nation is to pay more than 25 percent of the organization's total budget and no nation is to pay less than 0.01 percent. The only nation presently obliged to pay 25 percent is the United States.

Beyond the regular budget, there are extra assessments made to help with various emergency actions of U.N. forces around the world. Other activities of the United Nations are financed by voluntary contributions. Those special programs include, for example, the Office of the United Nations High Commissioner for Refugees, the World Food Program, and the United Nations Children's Fund.

Overall, the financing of U.N. operations remains a serious problem. In view of the heightened role of the United Nations as "the last best hope of humanity" for world peace, it is unfortunate that many nations still are unable—or unwilling—to pay their share of the organization's expenses.

In the future, budgets will probably rise, particularly if more peacekeeping operations come into play. Additional money will almost certainly be needed, therefore, to make possible the continued performance of United Nations actions.

4

Years of Triumph and Tragedy: The United Nations as International Peacemaker

> The world no longer has a choice between force and law. If civilization is to survive, it must choose the rule of law.
>
> —*Dwight D. Eisenhower*

Most of the first half-century in the history of the United Nations took place during the Cold War—the struggle for world leadership between the Communist nations, led by the Soviet Union, and the Western powers, led by the United States of America.

As a result, from its very birth in 1945 the United Nations was caught in the middle of the bitter competition. Instead of simply attempting to serve as the world's police force, pouring water over fires that broke out in the form of conflicts between neighboring countries, the United Nations also had to deal with a larger problem. Which of the two great power blocs would it be that eventually might organize the planet?

Since the late 1980s, Soviet power has crumbled. All of Eastern Europe—Hungary, Romania, Bulgaria, and Czechoslovakia—has split away from the once-dominant USSR. East

41

Germany, a powerful Soviet ally, joined with West Germany to form again a united German nation, a nation clearly allied with the Western powers.

Most important, the Soviet Union itself has been fragmented into many largely independent states, no longer dominated from Moscow by Russian power.

The former subject states of Latvia, Estonia, and Lithuania now are almost totally independent. Byelorussia and the Ukraine, a decade ago dependent on their Soviet "parents," now demand the right to chart their own course in world affairs and to support their own military forces.

Never is it completely possible to predict what may happen in the future. Historians seldom pretend to be astrologers. Still, by understanding what has happened in the years since the United Nations was first organized, we can gain a much clearer view of the way that nations have dealt with one another in an age when the possibility of nuclear war has always loomed as a threat.

At the same time, with such knowledge we can at least begin to project how a truly lasting peace might be secured in the coming century. That result—peace—seems possible if the world's nations actually begin to work together toward the goal of political order, something totally out of the question while the two great power blocs were engaged in deadly competition.

The purpose of this chapter, therefore, is to examine incidents of conflict during the fifty years since the creation of the United Nations as case studies, or examples. Those historical events may be useful in illustrating the successes and failures of a world body dedicated to addressing the issues of war and peace.

Then, by way of contrast, it will be interesting in chapter 6 to focus specifically on actions of the United Nations since the decline of the once-powerful Communist bloc of nations.

For the years of the Cold War, two incidents particularly stand out as illustrations of peacekeeping difficulties experienced by the United Nations: first the Korean War; and, second, the series of conflicts relating to the creation and survival of the State of Israel. Finally, we should conclude by noting briefly some additional examples of U.N. actions.

The Korean War

During the decades of conflict between East and West known as the Cold War, the United Nations participated most fully in one extended and costly struggle against aggression—the Korean War.

In August 1945, as World War II was drawing to a close, the Soviet Union suddenly declared war against Japan, sending massive numbers of troops into the Japanese-controlled peninsula of Korea. The United States objected strongly to the Soviet seizure of such important territory. Instead, the Americans persuaded the Soviets to retreat to the north of the thirty-eighth parallel, thus dividing the Korean nation roughly in half.

Two years later the United States, eager to withdraw its troops from South Korea, proposed a national election. After the election, both American and Soviet troops would be withdrawn. The USSR, however, rejected the proposal. The Cold War, led by the two superpowers, now stood firmly in the way of Korea's unification.

In August 1948 the United States went ahead with the election. Then, in spite of warnings from Syngman Rhee, president of the newly formed Republic of Korea, the United States withdrew almost all of its troops from the peninsula.

Shortly afterward, Chairman Mao Tse-tung of China traveled to Moscow to meet with the Soviet leader, Joseph Stalin. The

Soviets soon began to withdraw their forces from North Korea, leaving behind a well-trained Korean army equipped with highly advanced technical weaponry.

In January 1949 the American secretary of state, Dean Acheson, declared in a speech that Korea lay outside the defensive lines set up by the United States against Soviet aggression. Nations in such a position, he said, should eventually depend on protection from the United Nations and the entire civilized world, not just on the United States. Meanwhile, however, they must be prepared to defend *themselves* from attack.

That statement may have proved costly. On June 25, 1950, North Korean troops stormed across the thirty-eighth parallel in a devastating attack on the South.

Immediately after hearing of the invasion, U.N. Secretary-General Trygve Lie sharply condemned the action as a violation of the United Nations Charter and a serious threat to world peace. The Soviet Union and other Communist nations, said Lie, must either support once again the peaceful settlement of disputes or else establish their own organization of nations, apart from the United Nations.

On June 25 Soviet delegates temporarily stayed away from sessions of the Security Council to protest that organization's failure to seat the new Communist government of China, victorious over the Chinese Nationalists. Thus, without the danger of a Soviet veto, the Security Council passed resolutions calling for a cease-fire and the withdrawal of North Korean troops from the South.

On July 7 the council passed a resolution supporting the use of the United Nations flag as well as the choice of an American, General Douglas MacArthur, as leader of the United Nations force opposing the invasion.

Realizing their mistake, the Soviets returned in August to

A Canadian rifleman is helped to an aid station near the front lines during a battle in Korea in 1951. *Army Photo / United Nations.*

sessions of the Security Council. They vigorously denounced the United States for "armed aggression" in Korea. They also attacked Trygve Lie for his support of the United States and tried to have him removed as secretary-general.

Sixteen U.N. member nations sent troops to help in the struggle against the North Korean invaders. More than half of the ground forces, however, were American, along with 85 percent of the naval forces and 93 percent of the air forces.

At first, following the attack by North Korean troops, the U.N. armies were pushed southward to the very tip of the peninsula. Then a massive counterattack brought them back once again to the thirty-eighth parallel.

After that, a vote of the U.N. General Assembly gave permission for the American-led forces to occupy all of North Korea, too. Under the command of General MacArthur, the U.N. force swept quickly northward, soon approaching Korea's border with China.

At that point, Communist forces from China crossed the Korean border and launched a massive counterattack, sweeping the U.N. armies back once again to the thirty-eighth parallel. Peace negotiations were started at Panmunjom, but the fighting continued for several months, with heavy casualties on both sides.

Meanwhile in the United States, much opposition grew to the frustrating conflict. Some militant groups argued that American troops were not permitted to use the full force of their advanced weaponry—including bombing raids against China and possibly even the dropping of atomic bombs. Other opponents argued that American involvement had already been too great in a foreign civil war fought thousands of miles away from the United States.

Surprisingly, the Soviet Union had been hurt by the war. If the Soviets had entered the conflict to help an ally, they would have found themselves fighting directly against forces flying the flag of the United Nations.

At the same time, many Americans and other free-world peoples were disappointed, thinking that the United Nations had not been strong enough in its actions. They believed, instead, that the Western alliance should organize its military actions through the North Atlantic Treaty Organization (NATO) and, the next time such a conflict broke out, act more decisively against the Communists.

An agreement is signed in Korea in 1953 by which sick and wounded prisoners of war on both sides are to be exchanged. Signing is North Korean Major General Lee Sang Jo. Opposite him is Rear Admiral John C. Daniel, USN, United Nations chief prisoner-of-war negotiator. *United Nations Photo.*

From the perspective of history, it could probably be argued that neither side really won. Still, the Soviet Union and its allies at least had come to understand that, unlike the era of the old League of Nations, aggression could not take place without at least the risk of retaliation by the democracies.

From the standpoint of the United Nations itself, many supporters of that organization would argue today that the army used in Korea really was not a U.N. force. Rather, it actually was an American force fighting to achieve American purposes.

The United Nations and the State of Israel

From 1933, when Adolf Hitler first came to power in Germany, until the defeat of the Axis powers in 1945, some six million European Jews were murdered. Some of the survivors managed to escape to such countries as the United States. But for others, the land they longed for most was the home of the Jews in biblical times, Israel, known at the end of World War II as Palestine.

For a quarter of a century Palestine had been administered by Great Britain, under an arrangement sponsored by the League of Nations. That British role at first continued under the new United Nations organization. But soon, after sometimes bitter conflict between Jews and Arabs over the ancient territory's future, the British decided to withdraw.

Arabs, representing some two-thirds of Palestine's population, demanded that the territory simply be turned over to them. There were other proposals, too, including the division of the land into Arab and Jewish nations—a plan strongly opposed by the Arabs.

In November 1947 President Harry S. Truman of the United

States spoke out strongly in favor of partitioning Palestine into two countries, one of them to be a newly formed State of Israel.

On November 29, by a vote of thirty-three to thirteen with ten nations abstaining, the United Nations agreed to that proposal, the Soviet Union supporting the American plan. Despite strong opposition within the Arab world and even within his own State Department, President Truman held to his position. On May 14, 1948, Truman gave the formal recognition of the United States to the new State of Israel.

The next day, May 15, Arab forces launched an all-out military attack on the new nation, vowing to destroy its Jewish population entirely.

Not until July 1949 did the fighting finally end. At that time, Egypt, Jordan, Lebanon, and Syria agreed to an armistice, although none of them would formally admit that the State of Israel actually existed.

But it did exist. It had survived the war and had done so, moreover, without military help from the United Nations—the organization that had voted to create it.

The truce between the Arab states and Israel lasted until 1956. During those years, frequent Arab guerrilla raids took place, most of them from bases in Egypt. Egyptians refused to allow Israeli ships to pass through the Suez Canal or to permit ships bound for the Jewish state to use that international waterway.

Then, on July 26, 1956, President Gamal Abdel Nasser of Egypt announced that his nation had taken over the Suez Canal for itself.

The British, who had built the canal during years when Egypt was under their control, were furious. So were the French.

Together, Britain, France, and Israel began planning an attack on Egypt.

According to the plan, Israel was to launch the attack. Then Britain and France were to enter the conflict, supposedly to restore order in the region but actually to regain control of the vital canal route.

On October 29, 1956, the Israelis attacked. The next day, British and French forces bombed Egyptian military bases. The British and French demanded the right to preserve peace and keep the Suez Canal open by occupying three Egyptian towns: Port Said, Ismailia, and Suez.

Egypt rejected the Anglo-French demand. Meanwhile, President Dwight D. Eisenhower of the United States privately expressed anger at the actions of Britain, France, and Israel, demanding that the three nations immediately withdraw from Egypt.

At the United Nations, America's usual enemy, the Soviet Union, joined with Eisenhower in calling for an immediate withdrawal.

Then, in the Security Council, Britain and France used their powers of veto to block the United States and Soviet moves. Soon after that, the debate on Egypt's situation was moved to the General Assembly under the so-called Uniting for Peace Resolution.

Only Australia and New Zealand joined with Britain, France, and Israel in voting against a resolution to halt the fighting. Despite that vote, some twenty thousand British and French troops joined with the Israelis in the Egyptian conflict, a struggle far bloodier than the two European powers had actually expected.

United Nations Secretary-General Dag Hammarskjöld finally determined to give the British and French a way out of the crisis. He proposed the creation of an international police force to supervise a truce. The two major powers quickly agreed to the plan.

On November 7, 1956, the United Nations General Assembly voted to establish UNEF—the United Nations Emergency Force—the very first example in human history of an international police force.

Fewer than ten days later the first contingent of UNEF troops landed in Egypt: some six thousand men drawn from Norway, Sweden, Denmark, Finland, Canada, Brazil, Colombia, India, Indonesia, and Yugoslavia.

Soon, British and French soldiers withdrew from Egypt. Israeli troops withdrew from the entire Sinai Peninsula, which they had successfully captured, as well as from the Gaza Strip, bordering the Mediterranean Sea. The UNEF group then spread itself along the entire 273-kilometer border between Egypt and Israel to prevent either side from attacking the other.

Although many public figures in the United States disagreed with such embarrassing treatment of Britain, France, and Israel, the result was peace—at least for a while. As a peacekeeping organization, the United Nations had scored a very real victory.

From 1956 to 1967 many violent incidents took place between Israelis and Arabs, particularly along Israel's borders with Syria and Jordan. Still, there were no major conflicts. Then, early in 1967, the situation began to change. El Fatah, an Arab terrorist organization, launched bloody raids from across the Syrian border. When Israel counterattacked, Egypt's Gamal Abdel Nasser supported the terrorists.

In May, Nasser moved troops into the Egyptian areas occupied by the UNEF forces. He then demanded that U.N. Secretary-

General U Thant, who had succeeded Dag Hammarskjöld, withdraw all of the UNEF troops immediately.

Without even putting the matter before the General Assembly, as the United States was suggesting, Thant ordered the U.N. forces out at once. Nasser then announced a blockade of the Gulf of 'Aqaba—Israel's only naval pathway to the Red Sea.

At 8:00 A.M. on Monday, June 5, 1967, Israeli units were suddenly notified that the Egyptian army had launched an attack. Responding in a carefully rehearsed pattern, the Israeli air force swiftly took to the skies, destroying more than four hundred Egyptian planes still on the ground.

Meanwhile, Israeli ground forces smashed to victory, taking the Gaza Strip and all of the Sinai Peninsula in battles to the south. In the east, they won a difficult battle for control of the city of Jerusalem and then succeeded in driving the Jordanians over to the east bank of the Jordan River. Striking northward, they also triumphed against the Syrians.

The Six Day War, as it was called, witnessed the complete achievement of Israel's territorial objective—national frontiers more secure than ever from Arab attack.

Following the swift Israeli victory, many observers at the United Nations expressed unhappiness at U Thant's rapid withdrawal of the United Nations Emergency Force from the Sinai and Gaza. That move, they suggested, had opened the way first for Egypt's threatening troop movements and then for Israel's devastating response.

The incredible Israeli triumph in 1967 took only six days. But it did not bring the lasting peace that Israel's people so desperately sought. Instead, there followed a period of trouble, primarily of guerrilla warfare—one act of violence after another.

The United Nations Relief and Works Agency for Palestine Refugees in the Near East provides shelter, food and medical services, and schools for displaced Arab refugees. Here a boy in a refugee camp in Jordan reads to his younger brothers. *United Nations Photo 156235 / J. Isaac.*

The situation also grew more complicated. Soon after the Six Day War ended, the Soviet Union signed a treaty of friendship with Egypt, agreeing to provide modern weapons and to help with troop training. But then, in July 1972, Egyptian president Anwar el-Sadat put an end to that treaty, believing the Soviets had begun to play too dominant a role in shaping his country's foreign policy. Sadat had also come to believe that new moves were necessary to force Israeli withdrawal from captured Arab lands.

In the years following the Six Day War, Arab terrorism against Israel continued to grow. At the 1972 Summer Olympic Games in Munich, Arab guerrillas killed eleven unarmed Israeli athletes, an act leading to Israeli air raids on guerrilla bases in Syria and Lebanon.

Then, on October 6, 1973, while Israelis observed the holiest of Jewish holy days—Yom Kippur—Egyptian and Syrian forces launched a furious attack, at first winning spectacular victories.

Soon, however, the Israelis struck back. In one week they managed to capture all of the Golan Heights in Syria, advancing to less than twenty miles from the Syrian capital city, Damascus.

On the Egyptian front, meanwhile, Israeli tanks crushed Egyptian defenses near the city of Suez and then smashed their way across the Suez Canal into Egypt itself.

At that point the Soviet Union sent a blistering message to President Richard M. Nixon of the United States. The Soviets went so far as to threaten the destruction of the State of Israel unless the fighting stopped. President Nixon first responded firmly to the Soviets. Then he dispatched a massive alert to American military units around the world. Quietly, however, he urged the Israelis to agree to a cease-fire.

Soon the fighting stopped. Israeli forces permitted U.N. supply trucks to distribute food, water, and medical supplies to the Egyptian military units they had trapped, as well as to the surrounded city of Suez. Before long the Egyptians and the Syrians, as well as the Israelis, agreed to cease-fire terms suggested by the American secretary of state, Henry Kissinger.

Once again, a U.N. Emergency Force separated Israeli and Egyptian troops. Meanwhile, beyond the Golan Heights, seized by the Israelis from Syria, the U.N. Disengagement Observer Force, linked to the U.N. Truce Supervision Organization, worked to separate the hostile powers.

In the years following the Yom Kippur War, tensions remained high between Jews and Arabs in the Middle East. Bitter wars also raged among Arabs themselves, including the lengthy conflict pitting Iraq against Iran. Israeli military forces continued to engage in direct clashes with the Arabs, often in response to terrorist raids against civilians from such areas as south Lebanon.

Still, occasional glimmers of hope sometimes appeared. In 1979 President Jimmy Carter of the United States succeeded in bringing together the prime minister of Israel, Menachem Begin, and the Egyptian leader, Anwar el-Sadat. That conference resulted in the Camp David Accord, leading to the exchange of diplomats between the two nations, as well as the return to Egypt of certain territories occupied by Israel.

Later, despite the strong anti-Israel bias of both the U.N. Security Council and the General Assembly, President George Bush of the United States succeeded in using the United Nations to bring Arabs and Jews together in face-to-face negotiations—something that had not happened in the previous twenty years.

In the autumn of 1991 talks were held in Madrid, Spain, and then were continued in Washington during the first three months of 1992. In December 1991 President Bush also succeeded in persuading the General Assembly (by a vote of 111 to 25, with 13 abstentions) to repeal a resolution it had passed in 1975 declaring that Zionism was a form of racism.

Still, Arab terrorists within Israel itself, as well as in Israeli-occupied territories, began to take an even more bloody toll of lives. Also, the radical Islamic terrorist group Hamas gained strong financial support from nations such as Saudi Arabia. That happened especially after an older group, the Palestine Liberation Organization (PLO), supported Iraq in its attempt to seize oil-rich Kuwait in the Gulf War of 1990–1991.

Some observers still held out hope for peace between Israelis and Arabs. Yet the Israelis could scarcely have been pleased to see Palestinians cheering during the Gulf War as Iraqi SCUD missiles slammed into the Jewish city of Tel Aviv.

A turning point in Arab-Israeli affairs was perhaps reached in September 1993, but without the formal assistance of the United Nations. Israeli Prime Minister Yitzhak Rabin and Yasir Arafat, Chairman of the Palestine Liberation Organization (PLO), concluded an agreement in Washington, D.C., supervised by President Bill Clinton.

The two sides agreed to sharply increased Arab independence in the Gaza Strip area along the Mediterranean coast, as well as in West Bank territories, beginning first of all near the Jordan River, in the ancient city of Jericho. Despite high hopes for peace, however, bloody fighting and terrorist attacks continued.

In the future, the role of the United Nations could be important, particularly in helping to break down the long-standing Arab economic boycott of Israel.

Other United Nations Attempts at Peacekeeping

From the time the United Nations was formed until the Soviet Union began to break up, the United Nations experienced only mixed success in its peacekeeping efforts. Still, there are important examples of the world body's attempts to search for peace— the activity central to its very existence.

India and Pakistan Clash for Control of Kashmir

When India became independent from Great Britain in 1947, one of the burning issues to stand out was that of Kashmir. Would the province remain part of India, essentially a Hindu nation, or would it join the newly created republic of Pakistan, predominantly Muslim?

In 1949 both India and Pakistan agreed to allow the United Nations to work with them to bring about a peaceful settlement of the dispute. But years of negotiation followed with little progress toward a solution. In 1965 bitter fighting broke out, followed by a truce and then, in 1971, even more serious warfare.

The struggle grew still more complicated when East Pakistan began to struggle for freedom from West Pakistan. The eastern part of the country—separated by some 1,100 miles from the western part and composed mostly of Bengalese Indians—suffered tremendous casualties at the hands of soldiers attempting to put down the rebellion. Powerful tanks and machine guns killed thousands.

When the U.N. Security Council failed to take action to stop the killing, troops from India attacked both East and West Pakistan. The Indian army won a tremendous victory. East Pakistan soon declared its independence, entering the world community as the nation of Bangladesh.

With the fighting at an end, it could clearly be seen that the United Nations had been unable to play a major role in bringing about a solution to the dispute. Meanwhile, far to the west, Kashmir, too, had come under even stronger control of Indian troops than before.

The Vietnam War

The struggle for control of Vietnam, involving France, the United States, China, and the Soviet Union, eventually proved to be the costliest conflict in money and human lives since the end of World War II. It also proved a tremendous embarrassment for the United Nations. That organization is said to have stood back "with folded arms," doing nothing, since, in the words of Henry Cabot Lodge, the U.S. ambassador to the world body, "it lacked the tools but fundamentally because it lacked the will."

United Nations Secretary-General U Thant tried actively to bring an end to the bloody fighting between North Vietnam and South Vietnam. But the United States, which had taken over from France in defense of the South, was confident of victory.

China and the Soviet Union, siding with the North, believed the American population would tire of the fighting and then demand U.S. withdrawal.

Neither side, therefore, welcomed the involvement of the United Nations. Some, including U.S. Secretary of State Dean Rusk, scorned the idea that the U.N. might actually be able to do something to end the fighting.

Still, as the struggle continued, President Lyndon Johnson became more willing to listen to U Thant. Finally, in 1968, at the urging of the secretary-general, President Johnson announced that the United States was putting an end to its aerial bombardment of North Vietnam. Yet the fighting continued.

In 1969 President Richard M. Nixon began removing some of the 475,000 American troops still serving in Vietnam, declaring his intention to "Vietnamize" the war. Peace talks continued—as did the fighting.

By the end of 1973 all remaining American forces had been removed. Without them, South Vietnam could not survive. On April 30, 1975, the South Vietnamese capital city of Saigon surrendered to Communist invaders.

The war at last was over. The mighty effort of the United States had failed. And, despite the deep feelings of U Thant about the conflict, for three decades the United Nations had played only a minor part in all that had occurred in the former French Indochina—Vietnam, Cambodia, and Laos.

United Nations Efforts Elsewhere

In the years from 1945 to approximately 1990, the first forty-five years of U.N. history, the organization found itself involved in a wide variety of conflicts, great and small.

In addition to those already discussed in this chapter, the United Nations helped, for example, to end a civil war in the Belgian Congo in the early 1960s. That struggle included not only African groups competing for power there, but Belgium itself and Premier Nikita Khrushchev of the Soviet Union. The restoration of order in the Congo, known today as Zaire, largely was the work of a U.N. peacekeeping force and the application of pressure by the United Nations to bring about peace.

To some extent, the United Nations was also involved in minor skirmishes in such varied locations as Bizerte and Granada, as well as the major struggle between Iraq and Iran in the Persian Gulf area. It played a part, too, in the quarrel between Greece and Turkey over the island of Cyprus, as well as in

Refugees from Vietnam arriving in Hong Kong. *United Nations Photo / J. K. Isaac.*

disputes concerning Nicaragua, El Salvador, the Dominican Republic, Angola, Mozambique, Namibia, Sri Lanka, the Philippines, and the Republic of South Africa.

In some of those cases the role of the United Nations was considerable, in others only slight. Still, the existence of the organization was real. To many people around the world it offered at least a hope for the future.

What lessons are to be learned from the actions of the United Nations during the first forty-five years of its existence, from 1945 to 1990—the years of the Cold War between East and West?

Most importantly, perhaps, the organization's efforts in

working toward world peace were limited by the struggle pitting the Communist world against the free world. In most cases, therefore, the actions of the United Nations were narrowly defined, limited. Clashes were subject to independent action either by the Soviet Union and its allies or the United States and its allies—or sometimes, as in Korea, by both groups of powers.

Since 1990, however, much has changed. With the breakup of the Soviet Union and the fading of Cold War rivalry, the task of the U.N. Security Council has grown enormously. U.N. peacekeeping missions have played a major role in the civil war in Somalia and have been highly active in Cambodia. The United Nations contributed much to tempering the bitter struggle in what once was Yugoslavia. It was the United Nations, too, that responded forcefully after the invasion of Kuwait by Iraq.

The involvement of the United Nations in these recent actions, along with a projection of the future—the possibility of some form of world government—will be considered in chapters 6 and 7.

First, however, chapter 5 is intended to examine the contributions of the United Nations to continuing problems on planet Earth: matters relating to international law, economics, global resources and population, as well as the continuing issue of human rights.

5 Pathways to Progress: The United Nations Specialized Agencies

> Internationalism does not mean the end of individual nations. Orchestras don't mean the end of violins.
>
> —*GOLDA MEIR*

When many people think of the United Nations, what first comes to mind are dramatic and often bloody peacekeeping operations, such as those in Korea and the Middle East. But there is another side to the United Nations. It is a side that few of us hear much about or find very exciting.

Yet, particularly during the years of the Cold War, when both the Security Council and the General Assembly often were paralyzed by East-West conflicts, it was the U.N.'s so-called specialized agencies that registered the organization's most significant victories—successes that helped keep the world body alive.

Among the more significant of those agencies, each with a specialized task, are the World Health Organization (WHO), the Food and Agriculture Organization (FAO), the International Monetary Fund (IMF), and the International Bank for Reconstruction and Development (IBRD). But there are many other

62

groups in operation, some of them having been formed during the era of the old League of Nations.

Eleanor Roosevelt, wife of President Franklin Delano Roosevelt and a leader in the early years of the United Nations, once described such important but unpublicized organizations as "the U.N. nobody knows."

This chapter is intended to describe the work of the United Nations groups, beginning with those in the fields of human rights and social problems; considering next the units concerned with "global resources," such as the environment, food, and population growth; and, finally, the organizations working in the field of international economics.

Human Rights and Social Problems

Human Rights

From the very time of its founding, the United Nations has been committed to the idea of human rights. The preamble to the organization's charter declares that the United Nations is determined not only "to save succeeding generations from the scourge of wars," but also to "reaffirm faith in fundamental human rights and in the dignity and worth of the human person." That goal, the preamble continues, is to be achieved "without distinction as to race, sex, language, or religion."

Such work was to be a primary purpose of the United Nations.

In 1946 the U.N.'s Commission on Human Rights was created. A part of the Economic and Social Council, it was headed for several years by Eleanor Roosevelt. Under Mrs. Roosevelt's guidance the group prepared a document, the Universal

Declaration of Human Rights (see page 112), officially adopted
by the United Nations on December 10, 1948. Ever since then,
December 10 has been celebrated throughout much of the world
as Human Rights Day.

Many of the world's nations still fail to protect the rights
listed in the declaration. Some countries claim they cannot give
people rights as long as their nations are poor, although it is not
clear how limiting justice might somehow produce greater pros-
perity.

Nor does the United Nations presently have very strong
tools for *enforcing* human rights—privileges that often differ
greatly in places around the globe.

What are the rights listed in the U.N. declaration? First,
there are matters relating to human liberty, such as freedom from
slavery or being placed in prison without a trial. Human liberty
also concerns freedom of speech, freedom of religion, and free
thought in general.

Next, the declaration defends people's right to political freedom: the right to assemble freely for the discussion of political
matters and then to participate directly in matters of government,
either themselves or through elected representatives.

Finally, the Universal Declaration of Human Rights says that
people have economic rights: the right to a job (not including a
job they are simply forced to take); the right to insurance against
unemployment when it occurs; and the right to care in old age
when they are no longer able to work.

To make the most of their natural abilities, says the declaration, people also deserve the right to an education.

Clearly, the achievement of such human rights differs greatly
from nation to nation. The way a person charged with a crime is
treated in the United States is quite different from the procedures

in countries such as Cuba, Burma, or Iran. Such differences may explain why the U.N. declaration was passed so easily. Still, in order to achieve closer relations with the Western world such nations as the former Soviet Union have signed agreements to respect human rights and then, because of changed conditions, have actually begun to honor the agreements.

It cannot be denied that some nations have agreed to human rights statements knowing full well that those rights will not be enforced. In 1965, for example, 110 governments signed a General Assembly motion, "Elimination of All Forms of Racial Discrimination." But how are such goals to be carried out? Although the highly idealistic language used by the United Nations may be helpful in keeping human rights goals alive, there is no way to be certain that any nation will live up to its promises.

Not surprisingly, the countries already guilty of human rights abuses work hard at the United Nations to keep the organization's programs small. Included among those nations are such leading powers as Russia, China, and India, along with Iraq, Iran, Syria, Cuba, El Salvador, Peru, and Yugoslavia. Some of the charges now pending relate to crimes including torture and executions.

There also are other kinds of human rights problems. They concern matters of health, education, and drug abuse.

Health

The World Health Organization (WHO) is a U.N. group committed to achieving a high level of physical and mental health for the people of the planet. It tries to achieve its goals by spreading knowledge about epidemics and infectious diseases, as well as about environmental problems. Among its aims are the setting of standards in all nations on such matters as the uses of antibiotics and vaccines.

In the past, WHO made major contributions to campaigns against malaria, tuberculosis, and venereal diseases. In 1979 it was largely successful in wiping out the disease of smallpox.

So far, however, WHO has been less successful in its campaign against HIV/AIDS, although it has engaged in active campaigns to warn the world's people about the problem. By the year 2000 it is possible that more than ten million children will have lost their parents to HIV/AIDS. By such actions as sponsoring a World AIDS Day in 1992, WHO has tried to involve more people by giving greater publicity to the very real dangers.

WHO has also been active recently in other campaigns. It has worked with nations including Belarus, the Russian Federation, and the Ukraine to prevent further nuclear accidents like the terrible Chernobyl accident. It has fought against the spread of malaria in Cambodia. It has also attempted to teach the world's people how best to prevent heart attacks and strokes, ailments taking the lives of some twelve million people every year.

Education

According to many scholars, it is ignorance and prejudice that have played a major role in leading nations into war with one another. This belief was an important factor in the creation of the United Nations Educational, Scientific, and Cultural Organization (UNESCO). It is stated in the UNESCO Constitution:

> that since wars begin in the minds of men, it is in the minds of men that defenses of peace must be constructed; that ignorance of each others' ways and lives has been a common cause, throughout the history of mankind, of that suspicion

and mistrust between the peoples of the world through which their differences have all too often broken into war. . . .

If wars truly begin "in the mind of men," then the process of peace must be deeply concerned with education. Yet the job is undoubtedly growing more difficult. It is estimated that the "youth population," 1 billion in 1990, will probably grow to 1.4 billion by the year 2025.

Meanwhile, lack of education is one of the world's great problems. In more than one hundred countries around the globe, the amount of money spent for education actually declined in the years 1982 to 1992, with a particularly sharp reduction in African countries.

In its early years UNESCO worked hard to spread world-wide understanding of cultural accomplishments by people in various countries: achievements in literature, art, music, science, religion, and philosophy. During the Cold War the organization made much of the need to develop mutual respect for the scholarly and artistic accomplishments of people in both the Communist and non-Communist worlds.

Beginning in the mid-1970s, however, UNESCO became interestingly tied to the Soviets and their allies around the globe. Instead of dealing with matters of education, science, and culture, the organization began to concentrate on questions of disarmament and the world economy. It made especially harsh attacks on the State of Israel (as have many U.N. agencies). In addition, UNESCO became intensely anti-Western, sharply criticizing the United States.

Under the influence of the Soviets, UNESCO also projected the view that nothing was wrong when a nation controlled and censored its media, using radio, television, and the press to further national aims.

The Western position was different. A free press, as in the United States, may sharply criticize what the national government does, informing the public of virtually anything that is happening. Nor, according to Western standards, should a government be able to deny journalists who criticize its actions the right to be heard.

UNESCO was not only attacking free speech and a free press, it was also spending vast amounts of money—some $300 million in 1984—a full 25 percent of that amount provided directly by the United States.

Angered by the huge expenditures of the organization and its strong anti-Western bias, both the United States and Great Britain withdrew from membership in UNESCO.

With the decline in East-West tension the body shifted its emphasis. It gave greater attention, for example, to serious problems in Asia, where childhood prostitution had increased sharply.

Still, the future of UNESCO, an organization originally committed to the highest of moral and intellectual goals, remains uncertain.

The Production, Sale, and Use of Drugs

In spite of efforts by the United Nations, drug usage has become a rapidly growing problem around the world. The United Nations International Drug Control Program (UNDCP) now supports more than 118 projects in sixty-seven countries to fight against drug abuse. The organization works particularly hard to limit the supply of drugs—helping poor farmers, for example, whose only means of survival once was the growth of drug-producing crops.

Yet, faced with economic problems at home, many nations—including the United States—were forced in the early 1990s to reduce the amount of money they voluntarily contributed to the United Nations project.

At the same time, some countries, especially in Latin America, have objected to United Nations efforts to strike at drug producers and sellers. According to complaints, such actions go beyond the rights of nations to control their own affairs, something written into the U.N. Charter. Still, there has also been considerable support for actions like the United States took in putting a halt to drug exports from Latin America.

It now remains uncertain what will be done in the future by the United Nations and by member nations to face this enormous problem.

Other Social Concerns

With the decline of the Soviet bloc, U.N. specialized agencies have increasingly devoted themselves to actions in the fields of human rights and related social issues. Among those matters now receiving special attention are:

- *the status of women*: assuring that equal rights for women will actually be achieved around the world.
- *crime*: international cooperation against individual drug merchants and organized criminal groups operating across national borders.
- *aging*: special U.N. campaigns to encourage nations to assist their older people, along with research on problems of health care for the elderly.
- *shelter for the homeless*: an attempt to assist member states in providing safe housing for the elderly. HABITAT, a U.N.

group, has supplied help to more than one hundred nations throughout the world.

Despite serious problems, then, in agencies such as UNESCO, it is clear that the United Nations has made important efforts during the first five decades of its existence toward the achievement of real progress in the struggle for human rights. Increasingly, a single standard is emerging for the treatment of human beings around the globe. The United Nations has provided useful information on what needs to be done, as well as models of how to do it.

Still, it is clear that some of the worst offenders among the nations have used the United Nations for their own purposes. In the setting of the United Nations they have viciously attacked the policies of such countries as the Republic of South Africa and Israel while themselves committing far greater crimes against their own and neighboring peoples.

Nor does the United Nations presently have sufficient power to act directly against nations that are abusing human rights, or to reward countries that are making progress.

In times to come, however, the high idealism that has gone into the U.N.'s programs may go far toward shaping sounder, healthier policies around the globe in the field of human rights.

The United Nations and Global Resources

Based on an examination of human rights issues, it should now be apparent that the United Nations is concerned with many problems other than war and peace, or "blood and iron." Along with matters of human rights, there also are serious challenges in the field of global resources—matters relating to the world's food supply, population growth, the environment, and the Law of the Sea.

Food

From the moment a baby is born, that child's very survival is dependent on somehow getting food. Yet, every day, half a billion people face the possibility of starvation. Unlike those who live in industrialized countries like the United States, a majority of people on planet Earth are poor—and hungry.

According to the World Food Council (WFC) of the United Nations, one out of every three children under the age of three

A child in famine-ridden Somalia holds out his cup for milk. *United Nations Photo 146504 / Peter Magubane.*

now living in the poorer nations is undernourished. Every day of the year some forty thousand such children die.

On the continent of Africa, some thirty million people, many of them refugees displaced by wars, are presently threatened with death by famine. In the former Soviet Union, billions of dollars in food aid are currently needed for people whose regular access to food supplies has been largely cut off.

The Food and Agriculture Organization of the United Nations (FAO) has expressed concern about severe food shortages in Iraq and Afghanistan, the sites of recent wars, as well as in Haiti, a country long short of even basic food supplies. Asia and Latin America also have serious problems with hunger.

According to FAO, however, the greatest threat of starvation is in southern and eastern Africa. Government corruption has played a part there, but rapid population growth and sharp military conflicts have led to continuing hunger in many countries on the African continent. Transporting food is an additional problem since the ports and railroads in some African locations are in poor condition.

Meanwhile, with the passing of Soviet and U.S. attempts to win allies in Africa, foreign aid to several countries has decreased. As a result, some farmlands have turned to deserts. Even in countries that have exported food in the past, such as Zimbabwe and the Republic of South Africa, there now are shortages.

In 1992 U.N. Secretary-General Boutros Boutros-Ghali supported the establishment of the Industrial Fund for Agricultural Development (IFAD). That group, FAO, and the World Health Organization (WHO) are all committed to reversing the situation in lands visited by hunger. They have tried to help poor countries with irrigation, as well as with money to establish new farms and fisheries. They have tried to convince a broader range of industri-

Villagers in Chad, Africa, enjoy the new water system they worked together to construct with funds from the United Nations Development Program and the Italian government. *UNDP / Ruth Massey.*

alized nations to provide funds for agricultural aid, knowing that today the United States supplies the vast majority of such financial resources.

The world's food situation continues to grow more serious. Clearly, then, something needs to be done soon. For, as U.N. Secretary-General Javier Pérez de Cuéllar once remarked, "Without progress in reducing hunger and poverty . . . there can be no real peace for millions of our fellow human beings."

Growth of the World's Population

The population of planet Earth now is about 5½ billion. If the rate of growth remains the same, by the middle of the twenty-first century, the year 2050, approximately twice that number of people will occupy the world—some 10 billion human beings.

Significantly, something like 97 percent of that population growth will take place in poorer Third World countries in Asia and Latin America, but particularly in Africa.

Unless something is done to change the situation, the poor will grow even poorer. Conditions will become far worse in such fields as housing, education, and medical care. More people will die of starvation. As a result, the potential for revolution will almost certainly grow.

Meanwhile, in the wealthier countries, birth rates have actually declined. In such countries, organized national efforts for family planning help to bring about the difference, along with the practice of choice by individual families.

During the Reagan and Bush administrations, the United States no longer gave strong support for world population control. At one point the U.S. Agency for International Development (AID) withdrew approximately one fourth of the American contribution to the United Nations Population Fund (UNFPA) because of money that group had given to China. Chinese policy demanded the use of abortions to achieve its one-child-per-couple goal.

Despite the promises of UNFPA to eliminate its contribution for abortions in China, President Bush refused to restore America's help to that organization. The United States thus remained the only major industrialized nation not to support the group.

At the same time, many of the nations suffering most from the population explosion have also refused to cooperate with the United Nations. The Philippines, Argentina, and other countries have completely rejected the U.N. program. The Vatican, too, has come out strongly against it. A few of the poorer nations, however, actually have introduced programs of family planning. Among them are India, Bangladesh, and Vietnam.

The Environment

Since 1972 the United Nations has sponsored many activities relating to the environment. According to one U.N. official long associated with the United Nations Environment Program (UNEP), "the stakes are high—nothing less than the survival of life on earth."

Serious problems exist today in places around the globe. There are matters relating to hazardous wastes, some of them dangerously radioactive. Vast areas, especially in Africa, are turning into deserts. Developing countries, also in Africa, are faced with the need to produce tremendously greater quantities of food to meet the needs of their incredibly expanding populations.

The world's remaining forests face increasingly serious dan-

A water pump in Senegal powered by solar energy. It was installed as part of a United Nations program to develop new sources of energy. *United Nations Photo 150182 / Sean Sprague.*

gers. The sources of fresh water around the world are threatened both by population growth and by industrial pollution. Oceans, seas, and coastal areas are threatened.

Meanwhile, the use of fossil fuels, such as oil, presents a serious threat to the atmosphere surrounding our planet. Already an ozone hole appears to be growing in the sky above, permitting radiation from the sun to do serious damage to human bodies. On the other hand, the reduced use of fossil fuels could cause serious financial problems for oil-producing nations, including the United States.

To meet such problems, the United Nations recently produced Agenda 21, an action plan to oversee future economic development on Earth while safeguarding the environment. That plan concerns a broad variety of issues, including human health, poverty, and population growth. All are factors that relate directly to the environment.

At a conference held in Rio de Janeiro, Brazil, in June 1992, governments cooperated to make Agenda 21 more than just a public relations statement. The U.N. secretary-general was given special responsibilities for following through on efforts to save the environment, working with U.N. agencies as well as with individual countries and nongovernmental organizations.

Although supporters of Agenda 21 are presently short of money to carry out their plans, they have at least taken some necessary first steps.

A related U.N. project is often described as the Law of the Sea. It involves the actions of member nations with regard to the world's oceans. When the original United Nations agreement was signed in 1982, many leading nations, including the United States, refused to accept its provisions. The U.S. has disagreed, for example, with one Law of the Sea measure that would require private companies that had developed oceanic technology to turn over their discoveries to competing countries and to other nations.

Presidents Reagan and Bush also opposed giving the United Nations the right to decide specifically who would be permitted to work on the ocean floor in international waters.

Clearly, matters relating to the environment are critical. The very future of our planet is dependent on them. Because of that, the United Nations may be asked to play an increasingly significant role in dealing with environmental issues.

The United Nations and the World's Economy

Closely related to matters of the environment are economic questions. For example, acid rain, the destruction of tropical rain forests, and the killing of endangered species of animals may have their origins in industrialized nations. But their effects can be much broader, having a truly international economic impact.

To deal directly with economic matters, the United Nations works through such organizations as the World Bank, the International Development Association, and the International Monetary Fund. Perhaps as many as 80 percent of all United Nations personnel are involved directly with issues primarily economic in nature. Most members of the international organization firmly believe that without a strong economy a nation cannot survive.

According to Article 55 of its charter, the United Nations is supposed to promote

    a. higher standards of living, full employment, and conditions of economic and social progress and development;
    b. solutions of international economic, social, health, and related problems.

In attempting to achieve these goals, serious conflicts have developed, particularly between the world's wealthier nations and the poorer ones, about just what the United Nations should do. Three paths to progress appear to have developed: (1) the gathering of information about international economic problems, (2) the creation of U.N. programs to help member nations deal with those economic problems, and (3) the negotiation of binding international agreements to help foster economic development. It may prove helpful to look briefly at each of these categories.

The Gathering of Economic Information

Although individual nations sometimes distort information they submit to the United Nations, the total sum of materials collected now provides the most dependable accounting of international and social data. U.N. groups such as the Food and Agriculture Organization (FAO) and the International Labor Organization (ILO) submit reports to the secretary-general, whose officers then process them and make them easily available. The United Nations also publishes such annual summaries as its World Economic Report.

U.N. Programs to Assist in Economic Development

Even before the end of World War II an organization known as the United Nations Relief and Rehabilitation Administration (UNRRA) worked to assist territories that had been freed from German and Japanese occupation. Not only did that group provide food and relief supplies, it also gave technical assistance in rebuilding national economies.

Since that time, a wide variety of U.N. agencies have played a part in economic development. Among them are the United Nations Industrial Development Organization (UNIDO), the United Nations Conference on Trade and Development (UNCTAD), and, of course, the United Nations Children's Fund (UNICEF).

Binding International Agreements for Development

In working for radical change in the international economic system for the benefit of poorer nations, one example stands out— and that one largely a failure—the New International Economic Order (NIEO).

At a special session of the U.N. General Assembly held in 1974, a group of Third World nations, acting with the strong support of the Soviet Union, managed to pass a powerful resolution. It demanded a radical agreement "to correct inequalities and redress existing injustices [and] make it possible to eliminate the widening gap between the developing and developed countries."

The NIEO program called for easier entry into Western markets for Third World manufactured products; higher prices to be paid for the goods from developing nations; sharp restrictions on major corporations in their removal of such resources as oil and precious metals; and a more important role for developing nations in such important international organizations as the World Bank and the International Monetary Fund.

The major industrial nations lacked the votes in the General Assembly to block the creation of NIEO. But, over the years, they forced the Third World nations to back down. A worldwide recession in the late 1970s caused industrial nations to import fewer goods. That left Third World countries with less hard currency income and a very real crisis in trying to pay their debts.

As a result, the underdeveloped nations changed their demands, pressing instead for cash advances, easier terms for debt repayment, and even direct economic assistance.

Today, many of the Third World countries are still discontented. But the breakup of the Soviet bloc, which had supported them at the United Nations, caused poorer nations to become more patient in calling for worldwide economic change. They now appear willing to move gradually to achieve their goals.

In working toward progress in human rights and a wide variety of economic and environmental matters since its formation, the United Nations has managed some success. What now remains to be seen is how the end of the Cold War—and with it the breakdown of a militant anti-Western power bloc—will affect the world, not only in terms of economic and social matters, but with regard to basic questions of peace and progress on this planet.

Those issues are the subject of the next chapter.

6

Decline of the Soviet Union and a Larger Role for the United Nations

We are all students, and our teacher is life and time.

—*MIKHAIL GORBACHEV*

In the years following World War II, it appeared for a time that the ambitious, well-disciplined rulers of the Soviet Union might succeed in their goal of organizing the political affairs of the entire world.

Communist leaders, not only in the USSR, but also in Eastern Europe, China, Cuba, and a host of Third World countries, held out to people the hope of a better life, a life filled with happiness instead of misery.

Instead, the Communist governments—supposedly the tools for shaping an ideal future—too often turned the dream into a nightmare. They frightened, jailed, tortured, and killed those citizens who refused to show loyalty—total loyalty—by obeying orders without question. In that sense they were little different from Adolf Hitler's fanatical Nazis, demanding the same kind of total obedience the Nazis had demanded of the German people.

Then, during the late 1980s, the tide began to turn. In

Eastern Europe, one after another of the Communist nations threw off the yoke of the powerful Soviet Union. Poland, Czechoslovakia, Hungary, Romania, Bulgaria, and East Germany declared independence from Soviet control.

In Africa, Asia, and Latin America, nations such as Angola and Nicaragua no longer chose to model themselves on the Marxist governments first structured by Lenin and Stalin of Russia.

Remarkably, the Soviet Union itself did virtually nothing to halt the crumbling of its world empire, built at such great cost in lives and money over so many years. Instead, the Soviet leader, Mikhail Gorbachev, applauded what he called *perestroika,* or the "restructuring" of the international community. In time, Gorbachev predicted, the entire world would become a place of peace, governed by "reason and logic" instead of war.

Why did Gorbachev do so little to prevent the breakup of the Soviet empire? Why, under his leadership, did crowds of citizens in Russian cities such as Moscow and Leningrad feel it safe to gather in massive public demonstrations while under Stalin even major public figures had lived their lives in fear of execution?

In part, Gorbachev was a more humane person. But there were other reasons, too. By the time he took power, the Soviet Union was a nation in deep trouble. Supplies of coal and iron, once great, were dwindling rapidly. Because of that, industrial machinery had to be brought in from other countries. The production of Soviet industry had slowed down. So had the nation's agricultural output.

Meanwhile, the United States and its allies in the North Atlantic Treaty Organization (NATO) were pouring billions of dollars into the creation of modern weapons—expensive new guided missiles, new bombing planes, new ships—all of them using advanced scientific equipment. With every passing day, the Soviet Union was falling further behind.

Gorbachev understood that unless he took action—truly drastic action—the USSR could not hope to hold its position as one of the world's leading powers.

So, the Soviet leader opened his nation to greater contact with the outside world, even allowing Soviet television coverage of life in the wealthy United States. He permitted public criticism of Communist party officials, including himself. He set free from prison such well-known critics of the Soviet government as Anatoly Scharansky and Andrei Sakharov.

In foreign affairs, he did nothing when one of the greatest symbols of previous Soviet tyranny—the Berlin Wall—came tumbling down. Every day afterward thousands of people from East Germany poured into West Germany, to freedom. Meanwhile, Gorbachev withdrew Soviet troops from Afghanistan, where they had suffered bloody losses in trying to support that country's Communist government.

Within the Soviet Union itself, the southern republics of Georgia, Armenia, and Azerbaijan, long uneasy with Russian domination, were given greater freedom. So, too, were the Baltic republics of Latvia, Estonia, and Lithuania.

It was also Gorbachev who eventually opened the way to independence for the nations of Hungary, Romania, Bulgaria, Czechoslovakia, and East Germany—freeing them from Soviet control.

In a larger sense, it is unlikely that, without the vision and cooperation of Gorbachev, such free-world leaders as President George Bush ever could have begun thinking about—dreaming about—the possibility of a "new world order," accompanied by lasting peace on planet Earth.

Clearly, such a dream is hard to achieve. But with the end of the Cold War, very real alternatives to armed conflict began to appear, options in which the United Nations would be called upon to play a far more significant role.

Not everything the United Nations attempted in the late 1980s and the early 1990s has been marked by success. Still, since the end of conflict between the United States and the Soviet Union—along with their allies—there have been notable examples of international efforts to achieve order and peace.

Between 1988 and 1993 the United Nations initiated a total of fourteen new operations—more efforts than in the entire first four decades of the organization's history. During 1992 the number of U.N. troops in the field quadrupled, while the organization's peacekeeping budget leaped from $700 million the previous year to $2.8 billion. Moreover, the U.N. forces were no longer confined to the task of merely separating conflicting armies. Increasingly, they have become "enforcers" of peace, actually involved in direct conflict to achieve international purposes.

As one case study of such action, it is useful to examine worldwide reaction to Iraq's invasion of neighboring Kuwait. Other recent ongoing examples of international peacekeeping include major U.N. actions in Cambodia, Somalia, and the former Yugoslavia.

Particularly in the massive effort in Cambodia, the United Nations was directly responsible for organizing peacekeeping efforts and shaping the direction of a nation's future. In Kuwait, the United Nations played a more indirect role, but one that proved highly significant.

Those two examples—Kuwait and Cambodia—clearly deserve our special attention.

Iraq's Invasion of Kuwait: The Gulf War

At 2:00 A.M. on August 2, 1990, Saddam Hussein of Iraq sent the massive forces of his nation into neighboring Kuwait. Within twenty-four hours that nation's capital, Kuwait City, fell to a tremendous assault by Iraqi troops and tanks. Iraqi invaders then moved swiftly to control the Kuwaiti oil fields and make their way toward the border of oil-rich Saudi Arabia.

In the rest of the world, particularly in America, in Japan, and in Western Europe, the price of oil immediately soared by five dollars a barrel and then rose even higher.

How would the affected countries respond, especially the United States—the only remaining superpower? Would other Arab states side with Saddam Hussein? And what role, if any, would the United Nations play?

In the months following the Iraqi invasion a host of truly critical lessons would be learned about international order, as well as about the new potential of the United Nations for responding to aggression.

On August 2, immediately after learning about the Iraqi invasion, President George Bush of the United States personally condemned the attack. More importantly, he brought the matter to the United Nations Security Council. By a vote of 14 to 0, with Yemen not voting, the council called for Iraq's immediate and unconditional withdrawal from Kuwait.

President Bush worked by telephone with world leaders for their support. Surprisingly, one of the powers to side with him, and with the United Nations, was the Soviet Union—always before that Iraq's chief supplier of war materials. Then, in an equally surprising move, King Fahd of Saudi Arabia agreed to the presence of U.S. troops in his country—including even women and Jews.

On August 7, 1990, Pr   he dispatch of
American ships, planes, a   ıbia as part of
Operation Desert Shield   were joined by
forces from Australia, Great ᴅ   ⹂anada, Italy, the
Netherlands, and a powerful Arab country— ⹂gypt.

Turkey cut off the flow of Iraqi oil through its pipeline, leaving Iraq's commerce in that product open only through neighboring Jordan. On August 10, thirteen of the twenty-one members of the Arab League agreed to provide military aid to Saudi Arabia to stand up against the Iraqis. Germany and Japan, not permitted since World War II to put combat troops into action, sent large amounts of financial assistance.

Meanwhile, the United Nations tried desperately to end the fighting in Kuwait and to prevent an even broader conflict, one involving many nations, from taking place. U.N. Secretary-General Javier Pérez de Cuéllar met in Jordan with the Iraqi foreign minister, Tariq Aziz, but with little success. Then, on November 29, the U.N. Security Council passed a resolution giving Saddam Hussein six weeks to withdraw his forces from Kuwait, establishing a deadline of January 15, 1991.

Saddam refused to withdraw.

Then, on January 12, both houses of the American Congress voted to give President Bush the authority to use force if necessary to end the Gulf crisis. Already, American aircraft carriers, fighter planes, bombers, paratroopers, and specialized groups had been gathering in preparation for action. So, too, had other allied forces, even including troops from the Soviet Union and such nations as Argentina and Bangladesh.

In all, approximately 700,000 soldiers would eventually face Iraq's army of 540,000 men. Against Saddam Hussein's 665 planes were some 1,650 from the multinational force. To face 174

The cars of Kuwaiti citizens destroyed by Iraqi occupation forces. *United Nations Photo 158169 / J. Isaac.*

ships from the world alliance, including 6 aircraft carriers and 2 powerful battleships, Saddam had virtually no navy at all.

On the night of January 16, the attack of the allied coalition began. Powerful missiles were launched from ships in the Red Sea. Allied fighter planes and bombers struck at Iraqi targets. Much of the world was stunned by the power of the attacks. Privately, American military officials admitted that, most of all, they wanted to avoid the slow buildup of force used by the United States in the Vietnam War. This time, there should be a massive operation leading to a quick, sure victory.

In response to the sudden attack the Iraqi air force—the sixth-largest air force in the world—managed only a token action. Many Iraqi pilots flew to safety in Iran, their country's longtime enemy, which was, however, opposed to such strong activity by the multinational force.

In the days that followed, Desert Storm, as the attack was called, grew even more powerful. Not only were Iraqi army bases and air-defense centers hit, but also oil fields, oil refineries and pipelines, and chemical-weapons plants. Sometimes, as in downtown Baghdad, bombs accidentally struck nonmilitary targets, including bomb shelters housing women and children.

Day after day the air attacks continued, preparing the way for the coming ground war in Kuwait by hitting at Iraqi tanks and artillery there.

But before U.S. General Norman Schwarzkopf, head of the allied forces, could launch his ground attack, Saddam Hussein struck back—not at the coalition forces devastating his country, but at Israel.

On January 17, Iraqi SCUD missiles plowed into the Israeli city of Tel Aviv. Other SCUDs, with poison-gas warheads, landed in Haifa.

What Saddam hoped such attacks would cause was immediate Israeli entry into the war. That, he thought, would lead Egypt and other Arab countries to withdraw from the allied coalition and to side with him. As the Iraqi attacks continued, President George Bush pleaded with Prime Minister Yitzhak Shamir of Israel not to strike back. Meanwhile, Palestinians in the West Bank area occupied by Israel stood on their rooftops and cheered the Iraqi bombardments.

The Israelis, under great pressure from Bush, stayed out of the war. Meanwhile, after Iraqi missiles did serious damage in

Saudi Arabia, many Arab and Jewish leaders actually came together in friendship against Saddam Hussein.

On February 24, five weeks after the coalition's air raids first began, General Schwarzkopf launched a powerful ground attack against Iraqi forces, not only in Kuwait, but in Iraq itself.

More tanks were thrown into action during that offensive than were used during the major battles of World War II. Within five days Kuwait City was liberated. Some twenty-one Iraqi divisions were devastated, thousands of the soldiers surrendering. Very soon, the remaining Iraqi troops were cut off from escape.

What Saddam Hussein had proudly predicted would be the "Mother of Battles" was over. The nation of Kuwait was liberated. It was a stunning one-hundred-hour ground victory for U.S. and coalition forces. President Bush quickly called an end to the fighting.

Still in power in Iraq, Saddam was faced with rebellions against his rule. But using his powerful Republican Guard forces, he brutally managed to crush the rebellions of Shiite Muslims in the south of his country and of Kurds in the north.

Clearly, Saddam understood that President Bush feared a power vacuum in the land of Iraq—a breakdown in government that could lead to invasions from such neighboring countries as Iran, eager for Iraqi oil resources. Hence, Saddam was allowed by the victors to stay in power.

What had been the role of the United Nations in the Persian Gulf War?

It had been the key to making the halting of Iraq's aggression an international effort—not just that of the United States and its close allies. Some thirteen Security Council resolutions had helped bring members of the world community together in the struggle

An Iraqi woman amid the rubble of a destroyed building. *United Nations Photo 158311 / J. Isaac.*

against Saddam. Although leadership undoubtedly came from Washington, it was the United Nations that had broadened the wartime alliance, even isolating Iraq from most of the Arab world.

In a major way, the United Nations had served as a unifying force, bringing together nations of widely different backgrounds—including former Communist governments—for the task of armed peacekeeping.

The United Nations Peacekeeping Effort in Cambodia

Whether actions such as that in Iraq will succeed in the future is, of course, uncertain. But it is clear from current United Nations efforts elsewhere that serious problems still remain following the supposed end of the Cold War.

Cambodia, once a part of French Indochina, along with Vietnam and Laos, serves as a useful illustration of the prospects for success in years to come.

The presence of the United Nations in Cambodia marks perhaps the most complicated and ambitious effort in the history of the world body. Beginning in February 1992, the United Nations became involved in the administration of that Southeast Asian country on a day-to-day basis while trying to bring back to their homeland some 360,000 refugees who had fled the country.

The agency responsible for the peacekeeping operation there is the United Nations Transitional Authority in Cambodia (UNTAC). That body is seen as important not only in helping a country in Southeast Asia, but as a model for U.N. actions in the post–Cold War era—the kinds of things that might be undertaken in a "new world order."

In 1978, with the backing of the then-powerful Soviet Union, troops from the neighboring Communist state of Vietnam invaded Cambodia. The Vietnamese caused the Cambodian leader, Pol Pot, and his vicious Khmer Rouge party followers to take refuge at Cambodia's border with Thailand.

In response, China sent forces into Vietnam to "teach the Vietnamese a lesson."

Despite the widespread and brutal killings of civilians that had been carried out by the Khmer Rouge, the United States objected to Vietnam's takeover in Cambodia. With American financial help a new group was formed, known as the Coalition Government of Democratic Kampuchea. Made up of the Khmer Rouge and two non-Communist groups, it was headed by Prince Norodom Sihanouk, Cambodia's head of state before the Communist takeover.

When Mikhail Gorbachev came to power in the Soviet Union, he cut off his country's aid to Vietnam. That act caused the Vietnamese to withdraw their troops from Cambodia and to work toward smoother relations with China.

But the answer to the question of who would rule in Cambodia remained unclear. It was then that the United Nations became actively involved in the crisis.

At a meeting on the subject of Cambodia held in Paris in October 1991 the United Nations formed a group to handle the nation's progress back to self-government. At an expense amounting to approximately $3 billion, a U.N.-sponsored force was formed. It included more than twenty thousand troops, police, and civilian administrators, organized as an "advance mission," preparing the way for the United Nations Transitional Authority in Cambodia (UNTAC). UNTAC, it was hoped, would be able to organize a free, democratic nation there.

With the passing of the Cold War from history, the Soviet Union and China, along with the United States, showed a new willingness to work together on the problem. They hoped to develop a peaceful, competent new government in the war-torn land.

In November 1991 the first U.N. forces arrived in Cambodia. They had three principal missions: to help keep order in the country, to assist in clearing hidden land mines, and to prepare the Cambodian people for national elections.

A Supreme National Council was organized, headed by Prince

Young soldiers serving with one of the four armed factions under U.N. supervision in Cambodia. *United Nations Photo 159185 / P. Sudhakaran.*

Sihanouk and including the Khmer Rouge as well as three other national groups. Sihanouk, the country's king and prime minister from 1941 until the Communist revolution of 1970, was chosen by the United Nations to lead the coalition because of his continuing popularity with the great mass of the Cambodian people.

UNTAC took responsibility for many aspects of life in Cambodia, including human rights, elections, and a wide variety of police and military matters. Although a shortage of funds proved a problem from the beginning, UNTAC became directly involved in such matters as education and health.

From the beginning, however, it was clear that military force would be needed to discourage the Khmer Rouge from trying to seize power once again. Hence the UNTAC troops made up the critical unit in the U.N. action. UNTAC was responsible, too, for arranging Cambodian elections and the new government's actually beginning to operate through a representative assembly made up of 120 members.

By March 1992 the first small group of Cambodian refugees returned from Thailand. Such progress was slow, however, since many refugees feared the onset of new fighting. Also, most of those who returned chose to stay close to Thailand—just in case the settlement agreement broke down.

Money to help the returning Cambodians also was a problem. They needed some kind of housing, as well as tools for farming or trade.

To pay for assistance to Cambodia it was assumed that the initial cost for the United States would be approximately $577 million, while the Japanese were expected to contribute as much as $1 billion. Other U.N. members, such as Britain, France, and Germany, have made significant contributions to the effort.

Along with help for returning refugees, funds from the United Nations also helped the Cambodians in the rebuilding of such facilities as public transportation, roads, schools, and health care centers. Former soldiers were given special education programs to help them succeed in civilian life, since it was believed they would no longer be living in a Communist society but one that, in many ways, would probably be capitalistic.

Still, the financial problems facing an independent Cambodia are bound to be great.

In the beginning, the most serious difficulty, of course, came from Pol Pot's Communist Khmer Rouge. In several provinces that group frequently broke its agreement of nonviolence, attacking forces of the other competing parties.

U.N. troops have been killed in encounters with the Communists, who even refused to let the United Nations inspect areas under their control. Nor has the Khmer Rouge lived up to the Paris Agreement, providing for the disarming of soldiers who had fought in the nation's civil conflicts.

In April 1992 Secretary-General Boutros Boutros-Ghali personally visited Cambodia to help prepare the nation for its forthcoming free elections. It was hoped that those elections and the Cambodian democratic constitution could make the former Communist state a model for other countries where, during the Cold War, there had been bitter conflict. Meanwhile, the United Nations promised to help the new Cambodian government with additional funds in the range of a billion dollars.

Unfortunately, following its defeat in the elections, the Khmer Rouge persisted in armed rebellion against the government.

In late September, 1993, Prince Norodom Sihanouk returned to power as king of Cambodia. At his side in the formal ceremony stood two men: his son, Prince Norodom Ranariddh, and the former Vietnamese-sponsored Communist leader Hun Sen. Both were to serve as "prime ministers" in a compromise political arrangement designed to prevent the nation from slipping once again into bloody civil war.

Although the radical Khmer Rouge still objected to the new government, U.N. mediators clearly had worked hard to achieve such an agreement and the establishment of political order in Cambodia.

In creating new national structures, such as that of Cambodia, the United Nations must face potentially great problems. Should U.N. assistance continue into the future, for example, with such matters as the Cambodian economy? What should be done, too, in the case of former despotic leaders such as Pol Pot and his chief aides, as well as with the Khmer Rouge military forces if they refuse to surrender their weapons?

By no means do such complex issues simply disappear. As a result, the final outcome of situations like that of Cambodia now remains unclear.

Such uncertainty also applies in fiery happenings in other locations around the globe, particularly in such countries as Somalia and the former Yugoslavia.

In Somalia, the leaders of rival clans reduced their nation to virtual chaos—total disorder and killing—until United Nations forces intervened.

In Yugoslavia, disputes among Serbs, Croats, and Bosnians (including Bosnian Muslims) extend far back into history, well before events there marking the outbreak of World War I in 1914.

Following the death of President Tito [Josip Broz] in 1980, the Yugoslav nation hung together tenuously for a time. Then it exploded into warfare as the competing national factions and religious groups tried to assert their rights to territories and to political control.

United Nations efforts to reach a peaceful compromise therefore met with opposition from groups that for so very long had hated one another.

It should be clear, then, that just because the Cold War appears to be over, there is no guarantee of permanent peace. There is no certainty that the United Nations will triumph and bring order to the world. Instead, the joy in the West that accompanied the breakup of Soviet power may prove to be something fleeting, and the peace short lived.

Yet the very opposite could also be true. The outcome of difficult situations in today's world may not always be followed by retreats into still newer conflicts or by U.N. failures. Instead, the events of recent years may truly mark a turning point in international relations.

From substantive U.N. accomplishments may emerge the basis for a new way of organizing the affairs of our planet—perhaps, indeed, a "new world order."

That issue—a new world order—fittingly will be the focus of chapter 7, the concluding section of this examination of the United Nations.

7

Our Future: The Coming of a New World Order?

> I have long believed the only way peace can be achieved is through World Government.
>
> —*JAWAHARLAL NEHRU*

One year in the late 1940s the national high school debate topic in the United States was: "Resolved: That the United Nations should be modified to form a federal world government."

World government! A seemingly impossible dream in those days of the Cold War, featuring the Communist bloc, led by the Soviet Union, in open confrontation with the free world, led by the United States.

But now, in the 1990s, much has changed. Many scholars, political figures, and "just plain people" around the world have begun to ask whether, indeed, it is time for a transformation in world affairs. Might it at last be possible to modify the United Nations, converting it into a world body with enough power to police planet Earth and secure lasting peace while not, at the same time, running the risk of a world dictatorship?

Is a just and lasting world order really possible? And, if so, how best could it be organized?

1. The World Federalist Position: Reorganize the United Nations into a Federal World Government

One organization in the United States, with connections to groups around the world, is known as the World Federalist Association. That group is committed to restructuring the United Nations and bringing into existence a form of new order in the world—a world government.

Many leaders have dreamed that one day a world government would be created, thus ending the devastating cycle of bloody wars that have swept across the face of the human experience.

In the twentieth century the League of Nations and the United Nations have seemed to many to be important stepping-stones toward such a unified government for the planet.

One particularly strong believer in world government, Emery Reves, prepared a useful summary of the World Federalist position in his book *The Anatomy of Peace* (1945).

According to Reves, the fall of the ancient Roman Empire led to total disorder—chaos. To protect themselves, people submitted to the rule of medieval lords and barons. But competition among those leaders opened the way to continuing wars and violence.

Once again seeking security, people turned to other rulers—kings—who attempted to create a new social order. Western religion, too, based on belief in a single God, produced for medieval people a sense of order in their lives.

In the eighteenth century came the American Revolution and

the French Revolution, both based on the idea of democracy—the free will of the people being held together within a country by law. From that point on, it was believed by many that nation-states might be based on the concept of individual freedom.

Some nation-states, however, acted in a very different way, preserving order by tyrannizing their people—as, for example, in Adolf Hitler's Germany and Joseph Stalin's Soviet Union. Instead of freedom, the result in such cases was barbarism, hatred, and destruction.

According to World Federalists, nation-states will continue in a kind of new feudalism, with warfare among those nations, until there is some form of world government. Then, when that larger unit of government is created, tyranny and war will disappear. Always before in human history there has been conflict—conflict between families, tribes, cities, provinces, nations. The conflict only ends when a larger unit is able to organize the smaller units, *regulating* them by law.

Federalists believe that, in the beginning, the nation-state marked a step toward human progress. That was particularly true in countries like the United States, beginning with the position stated in the Declaration of Independence:

> We hold these truths to be self-evident, that all men are created equal, that they are endowed by their Creator with certain unalienable rights. That among these are life, liberty, and the pursuit of happiness. That to secure these rights governments are instituted among men, deriving their just powers from the consent of the governed.

Hence, not one person—the king—but *all* people were to share in the process of government. Truly then, it was to be self-government.

At the same time that democratic nationalism arose, as in America, so too did industrialism. Nations looked for raw materials in other parts of the globe. They competed with one another for overseas markets. The result, particularly since the eighteenth century, has been conflict—with violence, suffering, and misery.

More than 180 nations now inhabit the earth, each one of them independent, each one of them looking out for its own self-interest.

Yet, as seen dramatically in the twentieth century, no nation can exist on its own. It is essential, even for the most powerful nations, to have markets in other countries for selling their goods.

Nor can those nations prevent aggression against themselves. Until December 1941 the United States had declared itself neutral in the war between the Axis (Germany, Italy, and Japan) and the Allies (Great Britain, France, China, and other nations). But when the Japanese attacked Pearl Harbor in Hawaii, the United States had no choice but to enter the conflict. No "world community" then existed to prevent such warfare or, once it had broken out, to end it.

By contrast, as the World Federalist Association points out, New York State does not go to war against New Jersey or Connecticut. Why not? Because they are part of a larger community—the *United States* of America.

No similar community of all nations exists, however, to prevent warfare among the countries of this planet.

One reason for continuing warfare, say those in favor of world government, is that there now is very little international law. Peace treaties may be signed to end fighting between countries. But the treaties are not laws, backed by force. When new problems arise, the treaties can easily be broken. Seldom is there a formally organized international police unit to support and defend people. The result is renewed conflict—war.

According to those who believe in world government, instead of diplomacy and treaties, it is essential to have law, order, and government—international law, international order, and *an international government.*

In local communities there are laws, courts, and police. So, too, according to World Federalists, there must be similar institutions for the entire world. Once that happens, a nation wanting peace—as the United States did in 1941—will not simply be forced into bloody conflict by a decision made in some other country's war council! National powers hoping to change their situations would do so not by attacking another state but by appealing to international law.

And what of the individual? Would citizens have less freedom or more under a system of world government? According to the World Federalists, there would be fewer wars and, because of that, more free choices for individuals.

It would no longer be necessary to stop producing automobiles and television sets every few years and, instead, be forced to manufacture dive bombers and machine guns.

Governments would no longer have an excuse to censor the content of newspapers and radio and TV broadcasts.

Nor would huge national debts be piled up, paid for by higher taxes, as the result of one war after another.

Similarly, according to those who believe in establishing a world government, if such a body existed, the people of nations around the world would find it easier to travel to one another's countries. There would be fewer restrictions on movement around the globe.

Then, too, with less money being spent on weapons, nations could spend more on housing, medical care, and schools.

Finally, according to world-government advocates, many of

A summit-level meeting of the United Nations Security Council in January 1992. *United Nations Photo 179195 / M. Grant.*

the conflicts that, for so long, have set national groups against one another would simply disappear. Today, for example, in what once was Yugoslavia, Serbs, Bosnians, and Croats fight viciously against one another. In India, Hindus and Muslims are bathed in blood. Czechs, Slovaks, Poles, Russians, Romanians, and Hungarians continue their long-standing rivalries. Yet in the United States, people of those very same groups go to school together, often even marry each other. The same is true of ancient foes, the French and the Germans, living together in Switzerland.

What brings such former enemies together in countries like Switzerland and the United States?

The answer, say the World Federalists, is some broader power—a sovereign government under which all the former rivals are now equal before the law. There is a larger mechanism—a larger power—that binds very different people together in harmony.

What is now needed in the world, as Federalist Emery Reves puts it, is "one unified, higher sovereignty, capable of creating a legal order within which all peoples may enjoy equal security, equal obligations, and equal rights under the law."

According to those who favor world government, the United Nations is an important stepping-stone, an instrument of change, that will eventually lead to a better world.

2. Other Suggested Alternatives to the United Nations

Not everyone hoping for peace in future years is in agreement with the World Federalists. Indeed, some political scientists are sharply critical of the idea of world government. One prominent international scholar who has expressed caution about transforming the United Nations into a world government is Inis L. Claude, Jr.

According to Claude, the act of giving a world government enough power to prevent war not only is unworkable, it also is dangerous. Why, he asks, would a major nation-state, such as Japan, Germany, Great Britain, France, China, or the United States, give up the right to act in its own self-interest? Would such states ever surrender the right to protect their economies against serious competition? And if they, or the weaker nations, actually disarmed—as believers in world government insist they must—how could they react afterward against a tyrant who somehow managed to take over the international government?

Alf Ross, another leading political scientist, remarks that since the beginning of human existence war has been one means used to seize things that people have wanted, such as cattle, women, or land. Like many other rulers throughout history, says Ross, modern dictators such as Adolf Hitler have craved three goals—kingdom, power, and glory. The search for those, especially for power, has led to war after war. That is because, in the past, such things could only be won by crushing every neighbor, every rival.

One way that nations have tried to prevent war has been through a "balance of power": alliances of groups of states against other groups of states. Such alliances, however, have not succeeded in preventing major conflicts, including World War I, when two alliance systems finally came into devastating combat.

Alf Ross sees arrangements such as the League of Nations and the United Nations as examples of the more desirable "collective security" approach to peacekeeping.

Yet even while those organizations have existed, nations have frequently gone to war to protect their national self-interest. There has been no guarantee that all other nations would join together in united action against a power that refused to obey the international body.

In today's world, for example, which nations may or may not cooperate to enforce a decision of the United Nations? And if certain powers join together in one case, as U.N. members did against Iraq in the Persian Gulf War, what guarantee is there that they will do so in other instances?

According to scholars like Ross, if a world government were established, there would have to be dramatic changes, including:

1. Total disarmament and the creation of an international police force.

2. An international court of justice to settle disputes between nations.
3. An international "congress."

Clearly, believers in world government differ widely on how much power such bodies might have. Would they only preserve the peace, or would they be able to go much further into the internal affairs of nations on such matters as race relations? Would there be a "world empire," or would today's nation-states still keep the power to deal with their own citizens, simply sharing powers with a new organization, one more powerful than the United Nations?

No matter how right and proper a world organization may be, the achievement of world government will not be an easy task. The necessary sense of community to bring it about on planet Earth does not presently exist. By and large, people still tend to think of themselves as citizens of a particular country. Religious differences, such as those championed by Arab nationalist groups, also stand in the way of a united world.

Even if a world government existed, there might still be serious problems. Would the members of an international police force, for example, think of themselves as citizens of the world, or really of India, China, Cuba, Germany, or the United States?

Then, too, what might happen if, instead of all nations being equals, one powerful government decided to take total power—to seize control of nuclear weapons and then to rule the world?

Such problems will not simply disappear. They are built into our world composed of competing nation-states. Still, significant events have taken place in recent years, most important of which is the breakup of the once-powerful Communist bloc of nations.

That development has opened the way to previously impossible peacekeeping operations by the United Nations in such locations as Cambodia and Yugoslavia. Beginning with the administration of Mikhail Gorbachev, the former Soviet Union has joined with the United States in a rapprochement—a coming together—in striving for world peace.

Since that time, the U.N. Security Council has taken on far greater responsibility for preserving world peace, a function assigned to it in the Charter of the United Nations.

It well may be that at some time in the future the United Nations will be transformed into a federal world government. Until that time, however, the present body continues to work for peace. Its organizational units are concerned with human rights, with trade, with health, with food, with education, and with a wide range of other matters needed to create a better world.

Because of those efforts, and in spite of all the problems it has thus far been unable to solve, the United Nations is an organization that clearly deserves to be honored.

Conclusion

Through much of the last five centuries of history the great drama of human life has been played out with *national* leaders as its stars. And those stars, by and large, have seen themselves as leaders of *national* causes.

Then, to maintain world peace after World War I, the League of Nations was organized and, following World War II, the United Nations took its place.

Yet not until the early 1990s was more serious thought really given to the possibility of what President George Bush once described as a "new world order"—a system calling upon all nations to work together to form a free, united world—a true community of nations.

It was the collapse of the Soviet Union, a dominant world power, that opened the way for the United Nations to involve itself in disputes all around the world. No longer do the Russians move to prevent Security Council sponsored forces from acting strongly in crisis areas. As a result, United Nations sponsored troops have participated in larger and larger operations. They have acted in crisis areas such as El Salvador, Angola, Yugoslavia,

Cambodia, Kuwait, and Somalia, with monetary costs skyrocketing into the billions of dollars.

Meanwhile, citizens in the former Soviet Union and the nations of Eastern Europe increasingly are free to move about and to express themselves. They have greater freedom to work for money that they are actually allowed to keep. They have opportunities to choose their own jobs and to elect their own leaders.

At the same time, in the United States and other countries of the free world, governments are trying to make certain that the hopes of people are met for such basic needs as education, jobs, and medical care—elements that are supposed to be central to the dream, the ideal, of world communism.

Thus it would appear that, after years of bitter competition, the two main systems of government on planet Earth truly may be coming together.

Looking into the future of governments may call to mind a famous political story. It is the story of a desert society such as those that have existed for many centuries in North Africa and the Middle East.

In such societies, water sometimes is so scarce that it is like money. People fight and die over water. Arrangements for marriages are often made or broken because of it. Governments make war over it.

Some people live their entire lives in the desert. They know little about life as it is lived in America. Hence, they would scarcely believe that we have water fountains in our stores and offices, in our schools, even in the open—in our parks and playgrounds—and that the water is free.

If we were to talk to them, to tell them how much water we use, desert people might well become wild with laughter. They might slap their thighs and throw up their arms in disbelief. They would know with absolute certainty that either we were lying to them or that we were insane.

For after all, to them water is in such short supply that it is only a matter of "human nature" to struggle for possession of it—even to fight wars over it. For thousands of years people in desert societies have fought to have enough water.

But what about other societies, those like ours, where there is plenty of water? People in modern industrial nations, for example, have fought equally hard for other things—for money, for land, for glory, for power.

It may well be that we, too, have been living in a kind of desert, absolutely certain—completely convinced—that things in life simply have to be this way. It is, we are sure, only a matter of "human nature."

Or is it?

Since the creation of the League of Nations, and then of the United Nations, world leaders have begun to suggest that perhaps there may be a better way to live.

And now, at last, there are signs that without really planning it that way, human beings may actually be ready to come out of the desert, into a world of plenty—and into a world of peace.

If ever that truly happens, the role of the United Nations will have been crucial. For it is that organization that, somehow, has managed to represent the higher spirit of humanity in lighting the way to a better world . . . and a happier one.

Universal Declaration of Human Rights

Adopted by the United Nations General Assembly, December 10, 1948

PREAMBLE

WHEREAS recognition of the inherent dignity and of the equal and inalienable rights of all members of the human family is the foundation of freedom, justice and peace in the world,

WHEREAS disregard and contempt for human rights have resulted in barbarous acts which have outraged the conscience of mankind, and the advent of a world in which human beings shall enjoy freedom of speech and belief and freedom from fear and want has been proclaimed as the highest aspiration of the common people,

WHEREAS it is essential, if man is not to be compelled to have recourse, as a last resort, to rebellion against tyranny and oppression, that human rights should be protected by the rule of law,

WHEREAS it is essential to promote the development of friendly relations between nations,

WHEREAS the peoples of the United Nations have in the Charter reaffirmed their faith in fundamental human rights, in the dignity and worth of the human person and in the equal rights of men and women and have determined to promote social progress and better standards of life in larger freedom,

WHEREAS Member States have pledged themselves to achieve, in cooperation with the United Nations, the promotion of universal respect for and observance of human rights and fundamental freedoms,

WHEREAS a common understanding of these rights and freedoms is of the greatest importance for the full realization of this pledge,

NOW, THEREFORE,

The General Assembly

Proclaims this Universal Declaration of Human Rights as a common standard of achievement for all peoples and all nations, to the end that every individual and every organ of society, keeping this Declaration constantly in mind, shall strive by teaching and education to promote respect for these rights and freedoms and by progressive measures, national and international, to secure their universal and effective recognition and observance, both among the peoples of Member States themselves and among the peoples of territories under their jurisdiction.

ARTICLE 1.

All human beings are born free and equal in dignity and rights. They are endowed with reason and conscience and should act towards one another in a spirit of brotherhood.

ARTICLE 2.

Everyone is entitled to all the rights and freedoms set forth in this Declaration without distinction of any kind, such as race, color, sex, language, religion, political or other opinion, national or social origin, property, birth or other status.

Furthermore, no distinction shall be made on the basis of the political, jurisdictional or international status of the country or territory to which a person belongs, whether it be independent, trust, non-self-governing or under any other limitation of sovereignty.

ARTICLE 3.

Everyone has the right to life, liberty and security of person.

ARTICLE 4.

No one shall be held in slavery or servitude; slavery and the slave trade shall be prohibited in all their forms.

ARTICLE 5.

No one shall be subjected to torture or to cruel, inhuman or degrading treatment or punishment.

ARTICLE 6.

Everyone has the right to recognition everywhere as a person before the law.

ARTICLE 7.

All are equal before the law and are entitled without any discrimination to equal protection of the law. All are entitled to equal protection against any discrimination in violation of this Declaration and against any incitement to such discrimination.

ARTICLE 8.

Everyone has the right to an effective remedy by the competent national tribunals for acts violating the fundamental rights granted him by the constitution or by law.

ARTICLE 9.

No one shall be subjected to arbitrary arrest, detention, or exile.

ARTICLE 10.

Everyone is entitled in full equality to a fair and public hearing by an independent and impartial tribunal, in the determination of his rights and obligations and of any criminal charge against him.

ARTICLE 11.

1. Everyone charged with a penal offense has the right to be presumed innocent until proved guilty according to law in a public trial at which he has had all the guarantees necessary for his defense.

2. No one shall be held guilty of any penal offense on account of any act or omission which did not constitute a penal offense, under national or international law, at the time when it was committed. Nor shall a heavier penalty be imposed than the one that was applicable at the time the penal offense was committed.

ARTICLE 12.

No one shall be subjected to arbitrary interference with his privacy, family, home or correspondence nor to attacks upon his honor and reputation.

Everyone has the right to the protection of the law against such interference or attacks.

ARTICLE 13.

1. Everyone has the right to freedom of movement and residence within the borders of each state.

2. Everyone has the right to leave any country, including his own, and to return to his country.

ARTICLE 14.

1. Everyone has the right to seek and to enjoy in other countries asylum from persecution.

2. This right may not be invoked in the case of prosecutions genuinely arising from non-political crimes or from acts contrary to the purposes and principles of the United Nations.

ARTICLE 15.

1. Everyone has the right to a nationality.

2. No one shall be arbitrarily deprived of his nationality nor denied the right to change his nationality.

ARTICLE 16.

1. Men and women of full age, without any limitation due to race, nationality or religion, have the right to marry and to found a family. They are entitled to equal rights as to marriage, during marriage and at its dissolution.

2. Marriage shall be entered into only with the free and full consent of the intending spouses.

3. The family is the natural and fundamental group unit of society and is entitled to protection by society and the state.

ARTICLE 17.

1. Everyone has the right to own property alone as well as in association with others.

2. No one shall be arbitrarily deprived of his property.

ARTICLE 18.

Everyone has the right to freedom of thought, conscience and religion; this right includes freedom to change his religion or belief, and freedom, either alone or in community with others and in public or private, to manifest his religion or belief in teaching, practice, worship and observance.

ARTICLE 19.

Everyone has the right to freedom of opinion and expression; this right includes freedom to hold opinions without interference and to seek, receive and impart information and ideas through any media and regardless of frontiers.

ARTICLE 20.

1. Everyone has the right to freedom of peaceful assembly and association.

2. No one may be compelled to belong to an association.

ARTICLE 21.

1. Everyone has the right to take part in the government of his country, directly or through freely chosen representatives.

2. Everyone has the right of equal access to public service in his country.

3. The will of the people shall be the basis of the authority of government; this will shall be expressed in periodic and genuine elections which shall be by universal and equal suffrage and shall be held by secret vote or by equivalent free voting procedures.

ARTICLE 22.

Everyone, as a member of society, has the right to social security and is entitled to realization, through national effort and international cooperation and in accordance with the organization and resources of each state, of the economic, social and cultural rights indispensable for his dignity and the free development of his personality.

ARTICLE 23.

1. Everyone has the right to work, to free choice of employment, to just and favorable conditions of work and to protection against unemployment.

2. Everyone, without any discrimination, has the right to equal pay for equal work.

3. Everyone who works has the right to just and favorable remuneration ensuring for himself and his family an existence worthy of human dignity, and supplemented, if necessary, by other means of social protection.

4. Everyone has the right to form and to join trade unions for the protection of his interests.

ARTICLE 24.

Everyone has the right to rest and leisure, including reasonable limitation of working hours and periodic holidays with pay.

ARTICLE 25.

1. Everyone has the right to a standard of living adequate for the health and well-being of himself and of his family, including food, clothing, housing and medical care and necessary social services, and the right to security in the event of unemployment, sickness, disability, widowhood, old age or other lack of livelihood in circumstances beyond his control.

2. Motherhood and childhood are entitled to special care and assistance. All children, whether born in or out of wedlock, shall enjoy the same social protection.

ARTICLE 26.

1. Everyone has the right to education. Education shall be free, at least in the elementary and fundamental stages. Elementary education shall be compulsory. Technical and professional education shall be made generally available and higher education shall be equally accessible to all on the basis of merit.

2. Education shall be directed to the full development of the human personality and to the strengthening of respect for human rights and fundamental freedoms. It shall promote understanding, tolerance and friendship among all nations, racial or religious groups, and shall further the activities of the United Nations for the maintenance of peace.

3. Parents have a prior right to choose the kind of education that shall be given to their children.

ARTICLE 27.

1. Everyone has the right freely to participate in the cultural life of the community, to enjoy the arts and to share in scientific advancement and its benefits.

2. Everyone has the right to the protection of the moral and material interests resulting from any scientific, literary or artistic production of which he is the author.

ARTICLE 28.

Everyone is entitled to a social and international order in which the rights and freedoms set forth in this Declaration can be fully realized.

ARTICLE 29.

1. Everyone has duties to the community, in which alone the free and full development of his personality is possible.

2. In the exercise of his rights and freedoms, everyone shall be subject only to such limitations as are determined by law solely for the purpose of securing due recognition and respect for the rights and freedoms of others and of meeting the just requirements of morality, public order and the general welfare in a democratic society.

3. These rights and freedoms may in no case be exercised contrary to the purposes and principles of the United Nations.

ARTICLE 30.

Nothing in this Declaration may be interpreted as implying for any state, group or person any right to engage in any activity or to perform any act aimed at the destruction of any of the rights and freedoms set forth herein.

Important Events in the History of the United Nations

1939   Outbreak of World War II and collapse of the League of Nations.

1941   Signing of the Atlantic Charter by Roosevelt and Churchill.

1945   Signing of the United Nations Charter in San Francisco (June 26).

        Official creation of the United Nations (October 24).

1946   U.N. General Assembly meets in London, dealing with disarmament and peaceful uses of atomic energy.

        Trusteeship Council established.

        U.N. Children's Fund is formed.

1947   United Nations calls for establishment of the State of Israel.

1948   Universal Declaration of Human Rights adopted by U.N. General Assembly.

        World Health Organization established.

1949   United Nations arranges for Western nations to gain access to Communist controlled Berlin.

1950   During absence of Soviet Union from Security Council, resolution is passed requesting help for South Korea in reaction to North Korean invasion.

120

1953 Armistice in Korea based on U.N. sponsored proposals.

1956 U.N. peacekeeping force placed in Sinai after British, French, and Israeli success against Egyptians.

Soviet Union invades Hungary with no U.N. response.

1959 General Assembly adopts Declaration of the Rights of the Child.

1960 Large U.N. peacekeeping force works to end Congolese civil war.

1962 U.N. Security Council helps to prevent war between United States and Soviet Union over Cuban missile crisis.

1964 U.N. peacekeeping force sent to Cyprus.

1965 United Nations arranges cease-fire in Kashmir crisis.

UNICEF awarded Nobel Peace Prize.

1967 United Nations arranges cease-fire between Arabs and Israelis in Six Day War.

1968 Soviet Union invades Czechoslovakia with no U.N. response.

1971 People's Republic of China seated at United Nations as official representative of Chinese nation.

1972 U.N. Environment Program launched.

1973 United Nations arranges cease-fire after successful Israeli counterattack to Arab attack in Yom Kippur War.

U.N. peacekeeping forces stationed in Golan Heights and Sinai Peninsula.

1974 Turkish troops push aside U.N. peacekeeping force while invading Cyprus.

1977 Security Council imposes arms embargo on shipments to Union of South Africa.

1978 U.N. peacekeeping force sent to Lebanon.

1979 Soviet Union invades Afghanistan with no U.N. response.

1980 World Health Organization (WHO) campaign virtually eliminates the disease of smallpox.

Iran-Iraq war begins.

1982 Passage of Convention on the Law of the Sea by General Assembly of United Nations.

1983   U.N. involvement in struggle for independence in Namibia complicated by matters in neighboring Angola and South Africa.

1986   Following Chernobyl nuclear accident United Nations provides plans for assistance in future atomic incidents.

1988   United Nations helps bring about peace in Iran-Iraq conflict.

1989   Peaceful transition to independence from Soviet Union begins for nations of Eastern Europe.

Strong U.N. efforts to end apartheid in South Africa.

U.N. Security Council, with Soviet support, works toward peaceful settlement of conflict in Cambodia.

1990   Former Soviet satellites in Eastern Europe receive financial support from United Nations after their breakaway from Soviet Union.

U.N. trade embargo imposed against Iraq following Iraqi invasion of Kuwait.

1991   U.N. military mission arrives in Cambodia to supervise cease-fire.

United Nations imposes arms embargo on participants in civil war in former nation of Yugoslavia.

Resignation of Mikhail Gorbachev in USSR opens way to rule by Boris Yeltsin as president of nation known as Russia.

U.N. supported military mission is successful against Iraq.

1992   Large U.N. peacekeeping force deployed in Cambodia.

Peace accord signed in El Salvador with assistance of United Nations.

U.N. sponsored peacekeeping army proceeds to Somalia, preceded by force from United States.

U.N. Security Council prepares for possible major military mission in former Yugoslavia.

1993   Heightened U.N. efforts to bring peace to Somalia.

Heightened U.N. efforts to bring peace to former Yugoslavia.

Free elections held in Cambodia.

For Further Reading

An exceptionally large number of books have been written about the United Nations, including many for young readers. Those that have been most helpful in the preparation of this study are:

FOR YOUNGER READERS

Carroll, Raymond. *The Future of the United Nations.* New York: Franklin Watts, 1985.

Harrison, S. M. *World Conflict in the Twentieth Century.* New York: Macmillan, 1987.

Ross, Stewart. *The United Nations.* New York: Bookwright Press, 1990.

Vadney, T. E. *The World Since 1945.* New York: Penguin, 1987.

Woods, Harold, and Geraldine Woods. *The United Nations.* New York: Franklin Watts, 1985.

GENERAL WORKS

Baehr, Peter, and Leon Gordenker. *The United Nations: Reality and Ideal.* New York: Praeger, 1984.

Boyle, Francis Anthony. *World Politics and International Law.* Durham, North Carolina: Duke University Press, 1985.

Cable News Network (CNN). *War in the Gulf.* Atlanta: Turner Publishing, 1991.

Clark, Grenville, and Louis B. Sohn. *World Peace Through World Law.* Cambridge, Massachusetts: Harvard University Press, 1958.

Claude, Inis L., Jr. *Swords Into Plowshares.* New York: Random House, 1971.

Dunnigan, James F., and Austin Bay. *From Shield to Storm.* New York: Morrow, 1992.

Falk, Richard A. *A Study of Future Worlds.* New York: The Free Press, 1975.

Fawcett, J. E. S., and Rosalyn Higgins, eds. *International Organization: Law in Movement.* London: Oxford University Press, 1974.

Ferencz, Benjamin B., and Ken Keyes, Jr. *Planethood.* Coos Bay, Oregon: Vision Books, 1988.

Fosdick, Raymond B. *The League and the United Nations After Fifty Years: The Six Secretaries-General.* Newtown, Connecticut: Raymond B. Fosdick, 1972.

Franck, Thomas M. *Nation Against Nation: What Happened to the U.N. Dream and What the U.S. Can Do About It.* New York: Oxford University Press, 1985.

Gati, Toby Trister, ed. *The U.S., the U.N., and the Management of Global Change.* New York: New York University Press, 1983.

Harrelson, Max. *Fires All Around the Horizon: The U.N.'s Uphill Battle to Preserve the Peace.* New York: Praeger, 1989.

Henderson, Simon. *Instant Empire: Saddam Hussein's Ambition for Iraq.* San Francisco: Mercury House, 1991.

Hoffmann, Walter, ed. *A New World Order: Can It Bring Security to the World's People?* Washington, D.C.: World Federalist Association, 1991.

Kim, Samuel S. *The Quest for a Just World Order.* Boulder, Colorado: Westview Press, 1984.

Lie, Trygve. *In the Cause of Peace.* New York: Macmillan, 1954.

Moynihan, Daniel Patrick. *A Dangerous Place.* Boston: Little, Brown, 1978.

Reves, Emery. *The Anatomy of Peace.* New York: Harper, 1945.

Romulo, Carlos P. *Forty Years: A Third World Soldier at the U.N.* Westport, Connecticut: Greenwood Press, 1986.

Roosevelt, Eleanor, and William DeWitt. *U.N.: Today and Tomorrow.* New York: Harper, 1953.

Ross, Alf. *The United Nations: Peace and Progress.* Totowa, New Jersey: Bedminster Press, 1966.

Rubin, Jacob A. *Pictorial History of the United Nations.* New York: Thomas Yoseloff, 1962.

Stevenson, Adlai E. *Looking Outward: Years of Crisis at the United Nations.* New York: Harper & Row, 1963.

Tessitore, John, and Susan Woolfson, eds. *A Global Agenda: Issues Before the 47th General Assembly of the United Nations.* Lanham, Maryland: University Press of America, 1992.

Tompkins, E. Berkley, ed. *The United Nations in Perspective.* Stanford, California: Hoover Institution Press, 1972.

United Nations. *Basic Facts About the United Nations.* New York: United Nations, 1989.

United Nations. *The Blue Helmets: A Review of United Nations Peacekeeping.* New York: United Nations, 1990.

Urquhart, Brian. *Hammarskjöld.* New York: Knopf, 1972.

van den Haag, Ernest, and John P. Conrad. *The U.N., In or Out?* New York: Plenum, 1987.

Waldheim, Kurt. *In the Eye of the Storm: A Memoir.* Bethesda, Maryland: Adler & Adler, 1986.

NOTE: The final story in this book, concerning conflicts over water in a desert society, first was made popular by Professor Michael Harrington of Queens College, City University of New York. Professor Harrington devoted his entire career to showing people how a caring, feeling government might help them to live better, happier lives.

Index